No Paws Left Behind

C. S. Huxley

No Paws Left Behind, published April, 2022

Editorial and proofreading services: Cath Lauria; Gina Sartirana
Interior layout and cover design: Howard Johnson
Photo Credits: Front Cover: Outside Hamid Karzai International Airport
in Kabul, Afghanistan. Courtesy of the U.S. Air Force. Back Cover: White
House, photo by Vacclav, Getty Images/iStockphoto

 **SDP Publishing**

Published by SDP Publishing, an imprint of SDP Publishing Solutions, LLC.

SDP Publishing
Permissions Department
PO Box 26, East Bridgewater, MA 02333
or email your request to info@SDPPublishing.com.

ISBN-13 (print): 979-8-9856475-1-8
ISBN-13 (ebook): 979-8-9856475-2-5
Library of Congress Control Number: 2022905519

Printed in the United States of America

Prologue

Afghanistan

In the spring of 2020, a blond pup named Blue, the son of a brown Tibetan Mastiff and blonde Afghan hound, played with his dad under a pistachio tree, frolicking in the splendor of ankle-high grass and the first light of day. Wiggling to and fro, scratching his back, Blue snapped at a dandelion and barked as a pink cloudbank lit up the horizon. As the pink glow intensified, their play stopped, and all eyes focused on the inexorable sunrise. It was the first day of spring. A new era was dawning.

In the radiance of a Romantic sun, his mind illuminated with thoughts about the greatest sentient period in human history, Blue rolled over and met his dad's gaze. "So the meaning of a word is always deferred to the meaning of different words, and who or what dictates meaning has all power?"

His dad nodded.

"I want to talk to humans," Blue said. "We know a lot that they can't discern, like the fact that they're trapped in a language-thinking world which is used to control them. I want to free human attention from their language world."

3

"Dogs can't talk to humans," his father said. "That's the language golden rule for the ages, since Creation and Eden. We are humans' best friend. We don't engage in language word-games of deception for power. That's not our purpose. Our meaning is to be their best friend, truthfully and honorably. God gave us our meaning."

"What if God gave me a different meaning?"

"Blue, you'll find your own special meaning in the context of the grand meaning of life."

"What's the grand meaning?" Blue asked, furrowing his brow.

His dad snuggled up next to him. "It's a puzzle that involves many pieces: the will for meaning, internal freedom, goodness, a strange form of love, greater freedom for all, the ecstasy of infinity, and God."

Blue wrinkled his nose. "That's like a seven-dimensional jigsaw puzzle."

"Yes, it is. Remember, internal freedom and God are the most important pieces. Never forget the will for power and pleasure can work against the grand meaning."

"What else is important?" Blue asked, and rested his head on his dad's chest. "Wait, I know: attention, selective attention, and sentient consciousness."

"And what is sentient consciousness?"

"That's easy: smell, taste, sound, color, shape, number, motion, position, touch, vibration, pain, and sentient causality, or cause and effect. Mom taught me all about Sentio consciousness. It's where pictures and movies make meaning really fast in our brains."

"Very good, son. And remember love, the love given to another for their own freedom with no strings attached, the love that is doubly blessed for the giver and receiver."

Enjoying his dad's insight, Blue looked up at him. "That's like the kindness of strangers. Mom called it strange love. I remember."

"You've learned much from your mother."

Blue grinned. "But Dad, we could help humans with their struggle for power over one another if we could talk to them. That's what friends are for."

"Blue, you make me smile. We might help them in the short term, but by doing so, we'd destroy our ability to help them over the next thousand years and the next thousand years. By picking sides and engaging in human language games, we'd become worthless to future generations who face new derivatives of the same issue—the will for power gone awry. The side we pick today could become corrupted after tasting blood borne from power. Then they'll evolve into another species of the modern-day Progressive Socialists—only using a different banner for their deception."

Blue grew serious. "But Dad, I won't pick sides."

"What drives your need to help humans with their language-thinking?"

Blue shook his head. He'd never thought about what was driving his good intentions, but he knew his dad wanted him to examine his own will for power. Language was used like a weapon for power, but he'd be using language to help them.

Then he thought about American Progressive Socialists, who claimed everything their opponents spoke was racist, hoping to narrow their selection of words and meaning to their own socialist agenda, enslaving opposition to limited language thinking. It dawned on him. Language solutions for human political power struggles won't work. They'll only make things worse, driving human attention to greater language-meaning conflict.

He couldn't help his present human family if he argued about their political power struggles. In that moment, Blue decided dogs were here to direct human attention back to sentient reality, truth, love, freedom, and God.

Dad rolled him over, tickling his tummy with his paw. Blue giggled and guarded his loins.

Joining him in laughter, his dad released him, and Blue met his large, twinkling brown eyes and said, "When I grow up, I'll find a way to free humans from their language-thinking prison without using words."

1

Asha, the Afghan housekeeper, scampered down the stairs, ran toward the brown leather sofa in the great room, and grabbed the TV's remote control, tears streaming down her cheeks as she wept into her phone.

"Dari, it can't be true."

She was talking to the chauffeur. She flipped on the TV.

"No! No!" she screamed into the phone. "What are we going to do? We have no way out! And what about the animals?"

Liza, a ten-month-old black Labrador pup, and I had been playing "hide the ball" earlier, and were resting on the great room's floor when all the commotion began. Liza lifted her head, releasing the red ball, and gazed at me as it rolled across the floor. Her playful brown eyes were filled with uncertainty.

My ears perked up. Lying in my corner spot, I'd been half-asleep, enjoying the cool marble floor against my thick golden-blond fur. Now I watched images of chaos at the Kabul Airport flash on the flat-screen TV, which was propped on an old mahogany table. Then an image of a large Chinook helicopter hovering over the US Embassy in Kabul appeared on the screen for a long moment.

What the hell is happening?

More images at the airport showed US transport planes taking off with people clinging to the landing gear and falling to their deaths on the tarmac. Asha cried louder.

My heart pounded. I got up and shook my thick fur coat, scratched behind my ear, and gave a bark in concern. I hurried up the flight of stairs, Liza following close behind.

It was August 16, 2021, on Monday afternoon. We lived at house Number 9 on K Street in a suburb west of Kabul where embassy employees, their families, and their animals resided.

Mom and Dad, the two wisest dogs in the world, rested on their haunches on the hardwood floor in the playroom, their eyes glued to chaos on the TV screen above the fireplace.

Dad is a two-hundred-pound Tibetan Mastiff, nicknamed BB because he stands three feet tall at the shoulders and looks like a brown bear. His real name is Wise One, a name given to him by a Tibetan monk. Mother is an elegant Afghan hound with dark blonde fur named Rae, short for Rachel. Mom is in early pregnancy, and I look forward to welcoming my new brothers and sisters into the world, as do little Michael and Kim, John and Nancy Blair's children, the family who lives here with us. All four of them left earlier this morning and are at the US Embassy where John works,

Nancy teaches, and the children attend the embassy school.

I'm a two-year-old mutt about two-thirds the size of Dad. I have my mother's coat, her eyes, and my dad's face and paws. Dad named me Blue because, as a pup, I tried to chirp like a bluebird.

"What's happening? What are they doing?" I whispered as more images of people climbing over the airport wall materialized on the big screen.

"Panicking!" Dad replied.

"The people are frightened because America's Old Man is pulling out of Afghanistan in panic," my mother added. "The Taliban have control of all Kabul save the airport."

"I don't understand," I said. "Why?"

Dad glanced at me. "Kabul Airport is the only way out. Blue, this is all about political power and things that have happened over the last twenty years."

"What about Bagram, the grand military airport north of Kabul? We can all leave from there with our human family and the American military."

"The Old Man pulled out of Bagram and left it to the Taliban and ISIS," said Mother.

"Will little Michael and Kim be coming home?" I asked with a heavy heart.

"No, son," Dad said. "They've been forced to the airport. I heard Asha and Dari talking about their emergency departure."

Liza licked my face as I turned my sad eyes toward the hardwood floor. Michael and Kim didn't get to say goodbye to us.

My heart ached. I growled, then muttered, "Everything that Old Man touches turns to crap."

"Blue, control your temper and be respectful. John and Nancy voted for the Old Man," said Mother.

"What about us? What's going to happen to us?"

Dad turned toward me with a solemn face and shook his head. "I don't know, son. I don't know."

2

Three days later, on August 19, rumors were flying. An owl named Doctor Biggs, a huge Eurasian Eagle-Owl with orange eyes and a three-foot wing span, would visit and talk to my dad through the second-story, screened-in porch every day. Today he'd said the Old Man was going to leave Americans and their animals behind. The implications of a US military pullout meant innocent people and their animals would be left behind and murdered or starved to death.

Dad wasn't convinced by Doctor Biggs' message, which Biggs had claimed was direct from the Old Man's mouth. Dad wanted to hear direct from Colonel's mouth, who lived in house Number 7 on K Street. Colonel was a bomb-sniffing Belgian Malinois who lived two houses down from us, and he was the proud father of Conan, who'd trapped the ISIS leader al-Baghdadi, forcing him to detonate his suicide vest in 2019. Dad wanted to sneak out and visit Colonel tonight.

Taliban guards patrolled our street twenty-four-seven. They shot their brand new US M4 carbines into the night sky at all hours, rattling off thirty-round magazines one after another, as if they'd been given an infinite stash of ammo, and disrupting our sleep. Two streets over, baying beagles had rung out three nights ago, but we'd not heard them since. We believed the Taliban had killed them. Over the last two nights, I only growled, making sure to muffle my barks. I wanted to bark my head off to make the guards stop firing their weapons, but I didn't, fearing they'd kill us.

Dad was too big to go outside. Mom was afraid the Taliban would mistake him for a bear and kill him. Eventually, Dad conceded that fact to Mom and agreed not to go.

Liza and I had continued to play tug of war with a bone-shaped rope and "hide the ball" with our red rubber ball, making the best of our days in confinement. Occasionally, I'd stick my head out the dog entrance door in the back to sniff the breeze and feel the sun's warmth. Liza wouldn't stick her head out because of the beheadings reported on the news. Dad wouldn't let us go outside except when Asha or Dari took us out into the backyard to relieve ourselves.

Every day Asha made sure we had food and water, and Dari, a kind little man, would pet us while he talked with her about how they might escape. As the days passed, the airport seemed impossible as a way out of Afghanistan. There were too many Taliban checkpoints, and a massive unrelenting crowd surrounded the airport, blocking the entrance gates. Tonight Dari had discussed loading us into an old car and heading north. Asha knew we were rare and expensive dogs, and finally, she persuaded Dari that it would be too difficult to get us through all the roadblocks and inspections.

Asha turned on the TV in the great room downstairs, and all eyes focused on the screen as Usaria, an Italian commentator, questioned the Old Man about the August 31 deadline for the US military pullout of Afghanistan. We hung on their every word, and it was clear that August 31, 2021, was set in stone.

Near the end, the Old Man said, at Usaria's urging, that if all Americans were not out by August 31, the military would stay till all Americans got out. Asha told Dari she believed the Old Man was lying.

Dad got up from the marble floor and climbed the wooden stairs as Liza, Mom, and I followed him to the playroom.

"Will the Old Man keep his word and save us?" I asked.

"Family, I'm sorry to say that Lindsey, a patriotic mouse in the US White House, sent word that we are being left behind. His words were transmitted by a pigeon to dolphins, otters, sea gulls, golden eagles, and then to Doctor Biggs, who told me today," Dad said, glancing at Mom, Liza, and then me. "That's why I need to talk with Colonel. We can't trust what the Old Man says from one day to the next."

"You mean what the Old Man told Usaria was a lie?" I asked.

"I'm afraid it looks that way, Blue."

I was so upset I wanted to bark so loud the whole world would hear.

"Dad, Americans voted out a Trumpet who they feared was a tyrant, but now they've settled for totalitarianism. Seventy percent of Americans want us out before the military leaves Afghanistan. How can the Old Man deny Americans a voice?"

"Blue, it's not that simple."

"Did the Old Man win the US election?" I asked, shaking my head.

"Well, there was a long, coordinated pause on election night that has never been explained," Dad said. "And our friends—hawks, owls, and falcons—reported that people stuffed ballot boxes in the cover of darkness in major swing-state cities. Ballot numbers in various areas don't add up, exceeding the number of registered voters. Even the rats in Detroit, Atlanta, Milwaukee, and Philadelphia say the Old Man didn't win."

Feeling as empty and hopeless for humans as I'd ever felt before, I lowered my head. If America can't have secure and fair elections, then humankind's march toward greater freedom for all can't go forward. The banner of the self-righteous progressives, who cheated for their unrighteous cause, will lead to a totalitarian regime. I'd learned about tyranny listening to Nancy read *Animal Farm* to Kim. A Republic became a totalitarian regime under the banner of a power-hungry mob, led by a boar named Napoleon. The Old Man's regime believed they were the only way forward, so they cheated to consolidate all branches of power under a fake umbrella of equality, where they were more equal than their opponents accused of racism.

Raising my eyes, I met my father's countenance, now radiating confidence for the ages, glowing from his mane like a lion king. Dad nudged me with his nose, lifting my chin. "Freedom always wins. When a new freedom emerges, it triumphs."

Human history proved Dad's point. But this could become a Dark Age, where the Old Man's regime suppressed new freedoms. Nevertheless, Dad had sensed my hopelessness and always filled me with new ideas and hope for the future.

I smiled. "How can Colonel help us?"

"He has connections with the military," Dad said. "He'll know the truth."

I thought to myself, we can't stay here forever. We'll have to make a decision, and if the US military is pulling out, we'll need to leave too. The Taliban had killed animals on the street for target practice over the last two days. My family needed me to find the truth.

"Dad, I can get to Colonel."

"Blue, I don't want anyone going out there with those barbarians beheading humans and their animals," Mom said, and shook her head at me.

Dad looked at her. "Rachel, sweetheart, this may be our only way."

My mom knew, and I could see it in her teary eyes. She knew Dad was right.

Liza barked at me, wagging her tail. "I'll go too."

"It's better that Blue goes alone," said Dad.

"That's it, then. I'm going tomorrow in the early hours of morning when it's still dark."

3

Around four in the morning, I was ready as I'd ever be to find Colonel. I hustled through the kitchen where Mom, Dad, and Liza met me and told me to be careful and that they loved me. I told them I loved them, then I slipped out the dog door in the back of the house and padded softly like a cat toward the fence gate in the side yard. Approaching the gate, I noticed that the chain wrapped loosely around the gatepost wasn't locked. I gave a sigh of relief and used my nose to lift the fork latch, then pushed through the gate, moving stealthily in the cover of night.

Noticing one of the guards wore American night-vision goggles, I got down on the cool ground and wriggled through the front yard. I stopped twenty feet from four Taliban soldiers, armed with automatic weapons and night vision, standing beside a parked mini-pickup truck, blocking the street.

Terrified they'd see the green glow of my eyes, I waited with my eyes closed. A few minutes later, I peeked. The Taliban were preoccupied with an approaching car full of people, probably trying to get to the airport. I leapt to my feet and sprinted down the street to house Number 7 where a large X was painted on the front door. I hurried around back and gave a soft bark. Colonel didn't respond.

I walked softly toward the back door, sniffed, and could smell urine and dog poop. As I got closer to the flap on the door, a suffocating odor overwhelmed me. It was a combination of rotting eggs, spoiled cabbage, garlic, and human feces.

My heart pounded and, my legs trembled. I pushed through the flap and into a dark kitchen, hoping Colonel wasn't dead. A human head, severed from its body, was lying in a pool of dried blood on the tile kitchen floor. I barked in reflex and hurried up the stairs to my right, then a whimper emanated from a room down the hall.

I barked to acknowledge help had arrived, ran toward the sounds, and found an animal crate. Sniffing dried dog poop in horror, I tried to lick Colonel's nose, just beyond my reach. He opened his sunken eyes and moved his head, the half-dead golden Belgian Malinois weak as a kitten, dehydrated and starved. The door on his crate was zip-tied. I had to get him out.

The tie was pulled tight, so I worked to get my back teeth on it. Chewing as hard as I could, I broke through the thick plastic, and Colonel pushed through the door.

"Thank you, Blue. I'd have been dead by sunrise," said Colonel in a feeble voice.

"Save your energy. You need some water."

I led Colonel to the bathroom, stood on my hind feet, and reached to turn on the faucet, filling the sink with water. Colonel stood and lapped up the cool water. My heart warmed watching life spring into him. Then I thought about how horrible the soldiers were who'd done this to him. This was pure evil.

Colonel got down on all fours and looked into my eyes. "We've got to save the others. Those bastards beheaded Vijay because he'd helped Americans. They've gone door to door on a killing spree."

I walked close behind him as Colonel led the way to house Number 6 where we found George, a black and brown Rottweiler, zip-tied in a crate. I chewed through the tie and got George to water. In Number 5 we freed Teak, a feisty Yorkie, Duke, a large German Shepherd, and Mingus, a large gray tabby cat. They were severely dehydrated too.

I enjoyed setting them free, and felt a warm fuzzy from the experience of strange love like my mother had taught me. And I witnessed the effect of my love on them. They were so grateful. Mingus led us to his pregnant wife Molly, another gray tabby hiding in the attic. She was so happy to see Mingus. She jumped down to the carpeted floor and rubbed up against him, purring in joy.

In Number 4, we freed Harry, a Bengal cat with orange fur, black tiger stripes, and black-brown leopard spots. He'd been trapped in a small crate tied closed with a rope, which I'd destroyed in short order. Harry led us to Simone, a tan Siamese cat hiding in a bedroom closet.

It was getting lighter outside, and the sun would be rising in a few minutes. We needed to hurry. We ran to Number 3 and found Tiny, a large black Great Dane, chained to a wood column in the kitchen. He'd pulled so hard trying to escape that his neck was bleeding, and the chain had jiggled saw-marks deep into the wood.

We had to get that leather collar off Tiny. Colonel explained that I needed to get the collar between my teeth and bite as hard as I could. Tiny was weak and angry, growling as I approached his neck. I tried to explain first. Then Colonel calmed him as I carefully worked my lower jaw and teeth under his collar. I bit down as hard as I could, and Tiny growled louder. I couldn't penetrate the leather. I bit again with every ounce of power I had. But nothing. I released.

George approached. "Tiny and I are friends. Let me try."

Tiny lowered his head, and George worked the collar between his teeth. He clenched his teeth, and I heard a snap. He'd penetrated the leather. He relaxed and bit down again and pulled. His teeth had penetrated again. Colonel asked George to back away, and then he told Tiny to pull as hard as he could. Tiny pulled and pulled on the chain, and we heard the leather tearing. We cheered, "Pull, Pull!"

It popped, and Tiny was free.

Overjoyed, I barked in celebration. Mingus meowed, and we gave a thunderous round of barks for George the Rottweiler with the powerful bite. Tiny went straight to his water bowl and used his giant red tongue to lap up water faster than I'd ever seen. Smiling at the others watching Tiny, I noticed an odor from an adjacent room where there were two large bags of dried dog food in a mud room, plenty to feed our entire group, next to a large mop bucket filled with at least five gallons of water.

The sun rose over the backyard. Colonel and I told our group to stay here and stay out of sight for the day. Colonel and I headed back to Number 9 with the plan to return to Number 3 tonight. As we snuck back home and through the back door, I thought about how cruel

Taliban soldiers were. What they'd done to a big dog like Tiny, chaining him just out of reach of food and water, is what they'd do to Mom and Dad.

They were horrific!

Chapter

4

The next day, the Taliban marked the front door of house Number 9 with a black X. Asha put out food and water, enough for a week, and crying, she kissed us all goodbye. Dari and Asha left that night, traveling north to Mazar-e-Sharif.

Four days passed. Colonel didn't know what the US military had planned, because his contact had been killed. We'd spent our nights shuttling back and forth between Number 3 and Number 9, and we'd watched a lady on TV with purple hair named Suki, a spokesperson for the Old Man, lie about Americans being stranded in Afghanistan. Mother said that Suki insulted our sentient awareness with her language-world phenomenology and that she was gaslighting Americans. We'd held out hope over rumors that the US military would send squads from HKIA to liberate us, but that hope disappeared as more beheadings and public executions were carried out in our neighborhood.

Over the last twenty-four hours, I'd broken through my denial. Lindsey, the mouse in the White House, had told the truth, and the Old Man had lied to the American people and us. The Old Man's team was leaving their citizens, allies, friends, and animals behind.

Around seven in the evening, our entire troop of fourteen, including Doctor Biggs, gathered in the great room of house Number 9 to discuss options for how we might escape Afghanistan. Four cats sat on the brown leather sofa on one side of the room, including Harry, sitting at the front, and occasionally Harry paraded back and forth atop the backrest like a model walking down a runway. He'd been an active member in Cats Lives Matter, also known as CLM. He claimed their beef was that all dogs, since the beginning of time, had oppressed cats from becoming important members of society.

Harry cleared his throat and garnered the attention of the other cats, Molly, Simone, and Mingus. "I'm not taking orders from a dog, and that's final. In the past, dogs chased and treed cats, murdering many for no reason. I'll never trust a dog."

I sensed tension in the room after Harry had his say. Teak, another member of our company, was a proud Yorkie and member of Dogs Lives Matter, or DLM. Their group had formed in opposition to CLM, to stop the cats' power grab. Colonel, Duke, George, and Tiny gathered around Teak near the mahogany table and asked about DLM.

"Cats want to rewrite history," Teak said. "They claim St. Bernards never rescued any humans from avalanches in the Swiss Alps. They claim dogs are animal rights violators. Cats want dogs born today to pay for the crimes of dogs born in the past. They don't care about us. They won't change and will take whatever they can get. If we treat them with generosity, they'll take advantage of us.

"What's their goal? To replace us as humankind's best friend? To become God's chosen ones? No, of course not. They just want more food and power."

Harry raised his chin, turned his back, and lifted his striped tail as the group of dogs barked at him.

Dismayed, Mom and Dad watched the Harry and Teak spectacle unfold. Cats had better night vision than us. We needed them, and they needed us, if we were going to get out of Afghanistan.

Mingus, the large gray tabby, approached Teak, stopped, arched his back, and hissed.

Dad rose up on all fours, his head towering over everyone but Tiny. "Hear, hear! Give me your attention, please. We can work together for one purpose and under one banner that will underpin our equality and our mutual respect for one another.

"Our banner is simple: No Paws Left Behind. We'll not leave anyone behind. That I swear on my name and life," said Father in his deep, rich baritone voice.

The great room was quiet as Dad spoke, and I was proud of him. *No Paws Left Behind*, in essence, forms the basis of any society's foundation for equality. Dad had taught me that when one is sacrificed without consent in the name of *we*, then *we* becomes *they*, the bloodthirsty Progressive Socialist mob.

Doctor Biggs spoke up. "That's the best explication of what underpins our equality that I've ever heard. Even though I don't have paws, I'm proud to be a member of this team."

"Doctor Biggs, paws are just a metaphor for the equality of our essence and being in the world. Thank you for your kind words."

A lump appeared in my throat. I needed to speak up.

I knew this new basis of equality wouldn't work unless we all committed to it. I thought about the Old Man and his team, run by the purple-haired lady. They'd failed because they believed they were better and more equal than other Americans.

I moved toward Dad and addressed the troops. "Our banner of equality won't work unless we all make the same pledge as BB. Let's all stand and put our right paws over our hearts."

Harry shook his head and took a knee. Mingus stood on his haunches with his paw over his heart. Tiny joined, then Teak. All the other animals joined, and Doctor Biggs put his wing over his heart. Finally, Simone nudged Harry and whispered something to him, and he stood and joined us.

"Let us say before God and one another: No Paws Left Behind. We will not leave anyone behind. That we swear on our names and lives. Amen," I said, and the troop repeated it, then barked and meowed in a cheer.

Liza approached, wagging her tail with a big smile. She rubbed against my shoulder and licked my face. "I love you Blue. I always have and always will."

If I could've blushed, I would've. I looked toward Mom and Dad, and their grins were filled with pride.

On August 26, 2021, a suicide bomber penetrated the crowd near an entrance gate of Hamid Karzai International Airport (HKIA) in Kabul and detonated himself. When US Marines responded, gunmen opened fire on them. Initial reports were twelve Marines dead and fifteen wounded, with at least sixty Afghans dead.

Lindsey, a white-footed mouse living at the White House, climbed along an electrical cable in the ceiling, finding his way to the central overhead light fixture, the perfect place to provide a bird's eye view for eavesdropping in the Situation Room. The Old Man's regime was decked out in black, red, and yellow uniforms. In full Nazi-CCP regalia, Lindsey thought to himself.

Kline, Sallivan, Koby, Roani, Blank, Horrid, Suki, General McCow, and General George S. Ripper were all briefed on the attack at HKIA as they sat around an oblong cherrywood table, looking at each other in disgust.

"God dammit! God dammit! I told you this was

going to happen," McCow said. "We needed a stockade around the god damn airport and military police with bomb-sniffing dogs. Where the hell is the Old Man?"

"General McCow, calm down. General Ripper, we expected this to happen. Didn't we? This was priced into the evacuation," Roani said, garnering a nod from Ripper. "Let me remind you. This is all about perception.

"Suki, I want you to lead with, 'We expected this to happen. It's the price of getting out of this war.'"

"Let me remind you, Roani, that we look weak as crap on the world stage right now," replied McCow.

"You're right, General. We must retaliate immediately," Roani said. "Let's give the Americans some dead ISIS soldiers."

"Can't we just pay off the Taliban to execute a couple of guys and claim they were ISIS-K?" said Blank.

Horrid cackled like a hyena.

"Admiral Koby, what say you?" asked Roani.

"I think we should drone strike something and claim we hit the plotters of this suicide bombing. We'll call it an Over-the-Horizon hit."

"Koby, I like that idea," said Kline.

"Should we wake up the Old Man? We'll need his okay for a drone strike," said Ripper.

"I'll wake him," Horrid said, cackling again. "I love to see him confused as hell. It reminds me how close I am to the Oval Office."

"I'm going to brief China on what we're planning," Ripper said. "Zi likes to know what the hell the Old Man is doing."

"I'll contact all our media outlets and tell them to lead with, 'The cost of this brutal war will end soon, thanks to our President's great decision making,'" said Suki.

"Suki, tell Dorris and Zack, our social media puppets, to *suppress! suppress! suppress!* We don't want this Kabul shit to tank the Old Man's poll numbers any further," Roani added.

Lindsey scurried across the cable and ran to the roof. He wanted to get the news headed to Kabul. He needed to get the info to the coast, where dolphins could relay it through the Atlantic Ocean to the Indian Ocean and then to Karachi, Pakistan, on the Arabian Sea. He knew golden eagles would circulate the news overland to Kabul as soon as it got to Karachi.

Edith, a reformed stool pigeon, was eating birdseed on the White House lawn. Lindsey dropped a pebble from the roof, bouncing it on the sidewalk and gaining her attention. She flew up top, and Lindsey ran toward her.

"What have you got for me, Lindsey?" asked Edith.

Lindsey went on to explain, and she listened with great concern. She flew off on her way to the coast to relay the news to animals in Kabul.

Hurrying through the wall, Lindsey arrived in the Presidential Suite. It was there that he'd been dropped off with two other mice on Inauguration Day, January 20, 2017. Lindsey and the other two were lab mice from NIH used in Hantavirus research, a lethal respiratory virus with about sixty times the mortality of COVID. After being infected with Hantavirus on January 19, their saliva, urine, and stool stayed infectious for three days. Lindsey had survived while the other two mice had died that first week in the White House. Surprisingly, the new president and first lady had survived as well.

Lindsey found his bed but couldn't sleep. He loved America, and he wanted to save his friends from the Old Man.

Still cackling, Horrid knocked, then opened the door, and entered the Presidential Suite, pushing past the arms of two secret service agents. She stopped by the head of the bed with her arms crossed. Lindsey remained quiet peeking through a crack in the floor molding. The Old Man slept alone due to nocturnal flatulence, and he figured Horrid was about to get a noseful.

"Old Man, wake up and put your clothes on," said Horrid.

"What the hell for?" he asked as his eyes bulged in a moment of startling senility, and then he farted for several seconds, filling the air with an odor of a dead skunk.

"HKIA was attacked."

"God damn, can't you guys handle it?"

"We need your permission for a drone strike, sir," said Horrid, pinching her nose.

"Hell, I wish we could just nuke their damn Presidential Palace. But we need the perception that we're retaliating. Don't we?" the Old Man asked, his dull eyes filled with more uncertainty.

"Yes, sir. We just need permission to drone something."

"All right. You have my permission to drone something. Goodnight," he said, and belched.

6

O ur troop of equals met in sadness on August 28 in house Number 9. Many lives had been lost. HKIA bombing was all over the news. Initial reports were twelve Marines dead and fifteen wounded, with at least sixty Afghans dead. Updated reports were thirteen Marines dead and eighteen wounded, and ninety Afghans were dead. Colonel wept, looking extra sad, probably because he knew that if he and his team of bomb-sniffing dogs had been deployed at checkpoints outside the airport, this tragedy would've never happened.

I'd held in my anger towards America's Old Man out of respect for John and Nancy. But incompetence was still incompetence, and America's withdrawal reeked of incompetence. All those Marines, innocent children, and desperate people were dead because of the Old Man's bad decisions.

And if that wasn't enough, Doctor Biggs had gotten an update from Lindsey. The Old Man was going to launch a drone strike to give the perception that he was settling the score for the suicide bombing and then pull out anyway. I hoped he wouldn't kill innocent men, women, and children with his drone strike of deception. Things were bad enough without a blind drone strike and false narrative to promote the Old Man's image.

We gathered around the brown leather sofa in the great room.

"Colonel, we all feel the same way. This didn't have to happen," said Mother.

"Innocent women and children hoping to get to freedom were the perfect victims for this Taliban-ISIS massacre," said Doctor Biggs.

"Team, let's finish crying and get over this. It's time for us to go," said Harry.

My ears perked up when Harry said "team." That's what we'd become.

Dad walked to the mahogany table and gave options for our escape. Doctor Biggs joined him, explaining the perils of each option. Colonel added details about Taliban troops, wolves, and wild dogs.

We listened and shared our thoughts. Simone made some great points about getting assistance from other animals and friendly Afghans on our journey. We could live off the kindness of strangers, eating leftovers of lentils and bread.

Mom agreed not to vote, so there would only be thirteen votes to break a tie. We voted.

"That settles it," Dad said. "Iran, Turkmenistan, Uzbekistan, Tajikistan are a no-go. We'll head north toward Bagram and then east to the Nuristan Mountain Forest. Then we'll head southeast, follow the river to the Khyber Pass, then cross over into Pakistan near Peshawar, and move onward to the US Embassy in Islamabad. That's where John, Nancy, Michael, and Kim are residing, according to Doctor Biggs' latest intelligence."

The vote was unanimous. Our team wanted us to reunite with our family, even though it would be a treacherous three-hundred-mile journey through the Nuristan Forest, called a black hole by some and the dark side of the moon by others. Mom said that she'd visited the mountain forest as a pup, and she remembered seeing bears and wolves.

I headed out the dog door, and Liza followed. I needed some fresh air and time to prepare my mind for what lay ahead.

Under the starlit sky, Taliban fired US M4 carbines, rattling bullets into abandoned cars on K Street. Liza and I wriggled toward the two-hundred-year-old pistachio tree in the backyard, with two smaller trees on each side. It was my favorite place to think about things since I was a pup.

Silence fell over our neighborhood. We found some soft grass and rolled in play.

"How do you know so many languages?" Liza asked. "You understand Pashto, Farsi, English, German, and Mandarin."

"Nancy taught Kim, and I learned. I'm mostly interested in English and how words make meaning."

"How do words make meaning?" asked Liza.

"For most words, the meaning of a word is deferred to the meaning of different words, which drives the human power struggle to control meaning. You've heard

Progressive Socialists defer the meaning of their opponents' words to mean racism."

Liza wagged her tail to acknowledge.

"Some words make meaning through pictures, and some make meaning by emotions expressed with their use. Love said in anger can mean hate, for example."

"A never-ending deferral of meaning for most words," Liza said, lifting her head from the soft grass. "How convenient for the Socialist liars."

"It's worse than that. Language is being used as a weapon. Dictators and totalitarian regimes can control deferred meaning and beat their citizens into submission with their language meaning."

Liza's eyes opened wide. "Is that what's happening in America?"

"Yes. The Progressive Socialists are beating free Americans into submission by saying they are racists, terrorists, and less than their equals. Their mainstream media is reinforcing that narrative. Individuals can't fight back against the Socialists, and they are slowly being crushed, canceled one by one, like the character Winston in *1984*, the book John read to Kim."

Liza glanced at a shaft of moonlight, now lighting up the backyard, and then found my gaze. "What can we do?"

"I'm working on it. You see, words are supposed to be used to create pictures and ideas for creativity, efficiency, love, and freedom in the data-sphere of sentient consciousness. Instead, language is used as a weapon to control the masses via new laws and twisting the legal language of old laws into swords, turning concerned parents into terrorists for challenging government indoctrination of their children.

"I want to create a semiotic form of communication, one founded on an objective basis for knowledge like signs, objects in the world, and symbols like red meaning hot or stop depending on context, blue meaning cold, and green meaning go, for example."

"How would that work?" Liza asked, wrinkling her nose. "Individuals can't communicate with colors."

"The new method of communication needs to be natural and portable. You're right. I don't have the answer yet. I think it'll be pictorial, mathematical, binary, and musical communication combined like in the movie *Close Encounters.*"

Liza smiled. "That was little Michael's favorite movie. I remember." She hummed the theme from the movie.

I grinned, then looked up, and found the Big Dipper, then Polaris the North Star. I'd need to use the North Star to navigate on our long journey to Islamabad.

"Why should we care what humans do to one another?" Liza asked.

"What happens to humans will happen to us. If the power-hungry Progressive Socialists turn humans into soulless automatons who have forgotten the meaning of love and freedom, then they'll abuse us, forcing dogs to fight during hate week and torturing animals for fun, just like in *1984.* We'll all be lost and our meaning forgotten."

Tears appeared in Liza's eyes. "We won't let that happen on our watch."

My heart warmed at her genuine concern. "I love you," I whispered, and licked her face. We fell asleep under the canopy of my favorite pistachio tree.

8

S hots rang out from inside house Number 9. Liza and I awoke barking and confused. It must have been about four o'clock in the morning. I saw a flashlight's beam in the upstairs bedroom window where Mom and Dad slept. I heard more shots, then a truck motor sped away down K Street. My heart pounding, I ran inside, yelling for Mom and Dad. Harry approached, disheveled and breathless.

"They're gone," Harry said. "Four Taliban soldiers took BB and Rae on leashes, and they shot Colonel in the thigh. Dr. Biggs got away and is following them.

"BB told us not to fight them. They had US carbines and night vision. They would have killed us all."

Tiny, Duke, and George looked dejected. Their tails were limp.

I wanted to kill those Taliban soldiers. I was growling and showing my side teeth.

Liza came near, rubbed against me, and whispered, "You've got to calm down. Calm yourself, Blue."

I tried, but I couldn't calm down. I wanted to fight.

The house that I'd grown up in suddenly began to close in on me. It was hard to breathe. I barked and growled. Where were they taking Mom and Dad? What has happened to my family?

Looking around, I noticed the others appeared concerned about me and Colonel. I checked on him, and the bleeding had stopped. Molly, Simone, and Teak were licking his leg. The bullet had passed through his thigh without hitting any bones.

"I'll be okay," said Colonel, flexing his left leg.

Liza looked at me with tears in her eyes. "What are we going to do?"

"I'll figure this out," I said, ready to pounce on a Taliban soldier. I wasn't thinking clearly.

I'd never been this angry in my life.

George and Duke approached. "Don't worry, Blue. 'No Paws Left Behind,'" they said in unison.

Our entire troop joined in. "No Paws...."

I experienced the warm feeling of strange love. My eyes teared up. My thoughts cleared. I would give my life for my friends, and knowing that made me stronger. We'd become a team and now a family.

"Doctor Biggs will help us figure this out. He'll return with their fixed position. I know he will," said Harry.

I licked Liza on the mouth. She smiled. "No more tears."

Later in the afternoon, we'd still not heard from Biggs. Lying next to Liza in the backyard, my attention returned to the phenomenology established by the cruel Taliban. I could not free my attention from images of Tiny struggling for water and food, chained to a kitchen post in house Number 3. Pictures of Mom and

Dad chained to that post appeared in my mind, and I wanted nothing more than to kill everyone responsible for taking my parents away.

"What are you thinking?" Liza asked, and nuzzled me.

"My attention keeps bringing up an image of Tiny chained in the kitchen of house Number 3."

"What's attention?" Liza asked. "I know I can direct my attention. But what is it?"

I knew Liza was trying to distract me. I smiled. "Attention reaches out, grabs things, and holds them in brackets till we understand them."

"Where does attention come from?"

My dad had lived in a Tibetan monastery for five years. He knew more about attention, consciousness, and phenomenology than anyone alive, and he'd taught me a lot since I was a pup.

"Attention comes from external and internal sensory reception," I said. "It arises from sensory data-spikes in a part of your brain called the thalamus which sends out oscillating brain waves, called gamma waves, which move from the front to the back of your brain or, cerebral cortex, at forty to a hundred cycles per second, generating consciousness. Dad calls it thalamocortical dialogue."

"Wow! That's fast. So attention is preconscious," Liza said, her eyes twinkling.

"It's really fast, a hundred times a second. Attention is both before and within consciousness."

"Your dad used to live in a Tibetan monastery."

"Yes, he observed and learned all about this subject. Attention comes in two varieties: bare attention, as in passive awareness of things, and selective attention, as in focused on specific things. Ignoring their bare attention, Tibetan monks meditate and try to focus their selective attention, slowing down and increasing the amplitude of attention-gamma waves, while they get closer and closer to meditating about nothing."

"Blue, you know a lot about nothing too."

"It does sound like I know a lot about nothing."

Liza glowed from embarrassment. "You know what I mean. You understand a lot about attention and consciousness."

I grinned. "You're cute. Well, attention and consciousness are the keys to internal freedom. One's attention must be free to visit one's rich life experiences and God. Who or what controls attention builds one's phenomenology, controlling what one is and what one can become. It's important to exercise your selective attention and monitor your bare attention, making sure someone or something else like the media is not controlling it."

Liza's eyes filled with concern. "Your attention had you trapped in a bad memory about Tiny. What's phenomenology?"

She was right about my attention being trapped. And she'd managed to free it.

"Thank you, Liza, for freeing my attention. The images of Tiny chained in Number 3 and how I felt about the Taliban is my phenomenology of that scene. We'll talk about phenomenology later. It's the problem Americans are facing against the Progressive Socialists and their media attention drivers."

Liza nudged me with her nose. "Let's get some food and water. Doctor Biggs will be here soon."

9

Taliban soldiers had taken BB and Rae into the Presidential Palace and were holding them in a makeshift kennel of steel cages on a beige marble floor with black, red, and yellow oil-on-canvas paintings of mullahs hung on a canary yellow wall. BB was in a large cage, and Rae was in a smaller one, too small for her to stand up in. Doctor Biggs saw it all through a large window in the back of the palace after multiple flyovers. Taliban fighters had locked both cages with spring-loaded pin latches.

Doctor Biggs flew down, landing on a nearby tree branch. Hooting, he garnered the attention of a friendly local named Shelly, a brown Turkestan rat with beady ruby eyes who lived in the palace. Biggs explained the emergency, and Shelly listened intently, then spoke.

"Badass and Harkoni are the two main leaders of Taliban forces, and they're in a power struggle. Badass's forces captured BB and Rae. I saw them. They probably want BB as a palace watchdog, and they'll sell Rae's rare puppies. If Harkoni gains control, I hate to think what could happen. They'll probably murder BB and Rae because they lived with an American family," said Shelly.

He went on about how gruesome the Taliban were. He claimed severed body parts, including human heads, were kept in freezers in the basement.

He mentioned a big meeting tonight, a meeting to decide whether Badass or Harkoni had contributed more to the fall of America.

"Shelly, I need you there. We need to know what they are saying. Can you sneak in there?" asked Biggs.

Shelly stared at Biggs' orange eyes for a long moment and nodded. "I'll need you to drop me off on the roof after it gets dark. I can use an air vent to gain access to the attic. I'll access the main meeting room through a recirculation vent."

Doctor Biggs rotated his head 180 degrees, then rotated back. His eyes found Shelly's gaze. "Why are you willing to help us?"

"Maybe I'm settling an old score. I've heard what Lindsey the white-footed mouse has reported from the White House. Fuck the Old Man and his Taliban," Shelly said, and grinned. "Or maybe I'm just sharing a little kindness with a stranger."

"Thank you," Doctor Biggs said, and flapped his wings, lifting into the twilight sky.

Around eight in the evening, Biggs returned and gently lifted Shelly off the ground with his talons, flew around and over the palace, and dropped Shelly on a flat part of the roof. Biggs circled back and watched as he disappeared into an air vent.

Shelly shimmied down the air vent, accessed a central air duct, then scurried on top of the duct till he got to the main meeting room. He jumped to another duct and squeezed through a gap between the recirculation duct and vent connection, then found himself at the vent cover, which opened into the main room six inches above a dark tile floor and behind a brown sofa. The vent pulled the foul odor of unbathed soldiers toward him. He pinched his nose and took a deep breath through his mouth. He'd have to risk making a run to the sofa and then up the wall bookcase. It was the only way to see and hear what they were saying.

Shelly waited and waited, and when all the black and white turbans and robed soldiers sat, he dashed for the sofa. After a brief exhale and inhale, he darted toward the bookcase and reached the top shelf. He'd found a perfect position to see and hear all, hiding between one book entitled *QUR'AN* and another, *Arabs of Afghanistan.*

On the other side of the sofa, Badass and Harkoni sat opposite one another at a long table with many Taliban soldiers in chairs gathered around them.

"Praise Allah for America's Old Man, Secretary Blank, and General Ripper. Allah is good! He's delivered the weapons and money we'll need to destroy the West," Badass said. "We ask Allah to protect Harkoni and Abu Khan, the leader of our Pakistani Taliban brothers, also known as our enemies ISIS-K."

Harkoni and his soldiers broke out in laughter.

"America and their weak allies are fools and deserve to be destroyed. Their weakness is epitomized by the Old Man," said Harkoni.

"We must keep them believing. Keep the social media platforms on our side. Dorris and Zack, the media tycoons, are supporting the leftist power grab in America. They suppressed the Old Man's public laptop disaster, which documented his indiscretions. To the media tycoons, we are just a mistake they need to normalize to make the Old Man look good," said Badass.

"We think Ripper is in Zi's pocket. China's Zi must have a recording of him talking to his General Li, which proves Ripper is guilty of treason. Ripper will do anything to save himself, including betraying America. He hates America," Harkoni said. "That's the only thing we have in common with him."

"Yes, we'll lean on Ripper," Badass said. "We'll trap him; he'll have no choice but to help us detonate US nuclear missiles against their own people in honor of Allah. Ripper will trick the Old Man into a preemptive nuclear strike. Then when their new No-Horizon, No-Recall plan prohibits a recall, they'll have no choice but to destroy themselves to save the world from the Old Man's mistake." Badass paused for several moments and added, "We'll destroy America Osama Bin Laden-style!"

The Taliban soldiers erupted in cheers. "Death to the infidels! Death to America!"

Frightened by what he was hearing, Shelly slunk deeper between the two books. He realized that all this Taliban turmoil was just a smokescreen. They wanted to appear in opposition to one another, playing for more money and support from American fools. Of course, this was good news for BB and Rae. They were not in immediate danger. But it was tragic news for America. Ripper and the Old Man would become Taliban patsies and destroy America.

Long after the meeting ended and the lights were out, Shelly remained hidden out of fear, then finally hurried back, the way he'd come, to the top of the roof where he found Doctor Biggs circling overhead.

"What took you so long?" asked Doctor Biggs.

"It wasn't easy, and the meeting ran late."

"Did you find out anything?"

"Lots."

"Tell me," Biggs said, and landed on the roof next to Shelly.

"ISIS from Khorasan, or ISIS-K, is made up of disaffected Pakistani Taliban. Abu Khan is their leader and is a good friend of Harkoni. They are running a good cop and bad cop propaganda scam, pretending at times to be mortal enemies. It's all for show, to maintain a false conflict to trick the Old Man's regime to support Harkoni. Badass is in on it too."

"So Rae and BB are not in immediate danger."

"I would say they are still in danger, but not like I thought. Badass and Harkoni are playing games. They intend to use Ripper to confuse the Old Man and detonate nuclear missiles in America."

Shelly went on to explain the Taliban's elaborate plan to destroy America.

"You've uncovered some critical information. Thank you from the bottom of my heart. I'll be back tomorrow with some friends. We're going to liberate Rae and BB, and we'll need your help."

"No worries. I'll be here. Could you give me a lift down to that pine tree?"

Doctor Biggs gently lifted Shelly and dropped him by the tree.

"I'll meet you here tomorrow night at eight," Biggs said, and flapped higher into the air, heading toward house Number 9.

By around eleven that night, we'd still not heard from Doctor Biggs. Pacing back and forth in the kitchen, I waited anxiously while, once again, Liza tried to distract me. I didn't want to play tug of war or "hide the ball," though. I wanted to hit the streets and sniff my way to where Mom and Dad were being held.

"Blue, what is sense of being?" asked Liza.

I wagged my tail. Liza's innocence and curiosity had a way of capturing my attention. "When one's selective attention visits language-thinking consciousness, that's where you experience your sense of being," I explained, slowing my pace. "When you focus attention on sentient consciousness, attending to the smell of COVID or attending to the significant pitch of a human's COVID cough, that's where you experience your sense of being. Your attention-self reconstitutes in each now, now, now in language-thinking or sentient consciousness—thousands of times a day."

"How strange that we reconstitute so many times a day in now. So what is time?" Liza asked with smiling eyes.

"That's a tough one. Aristotle said time is what can be measured now-no-longer and now-not-yet. He had no way to measure now. Dad says time is experienced through the phenomenology of a series of sense-of being experiences and a summation of now-no-longer sense-of-being experiences which are re-experienced now.

"It's strange that now is where we experience our sense of being even if we are looking backward to the past or forward toward the future. I am worried about our future now. I'm sad about our past now. All we have is now," Liza said, walking beside me. "Your dad's a genius."

"Yes, he is. If your attention is not in immediate pre-reflective consciousness, like it has to be when sniffing for bombs, then you're reflecting on your past or future and not paying attention to the present. Most humans reflect all the time. That's why attention and phenom-enology are so important."

Reflecting about Mom and Dad, I led Liza upstairs and visited the playroom. Looking around at where they used to sit and talk, we heard a loud commotion.

Flapping his wings to slow his descent, Doctor Biggs blew in through the second-story bedroom window like a helicopter. Tiny, George, and Duke barked and hurried up the stairs with Harry to greet him.

"Where are they? What have they done to Mom and Dad?" I asked with urgency.

"Slow down, Blue," said Doctor Biggs. He could see that I was ready to run off into the night and rescue them.

"Are they okay? Are they alive?" I asked with a lump in my throat.

"BB and Rae are okay. We'll rescue them tomorrow night. They're in the Presidential Palace."

My heart stopped when I heard where they were. That palace was like a concrete fortress with a medieval turret, surrounded by a hundred Taliban guards in the middle of Kabul.

Doctor Biggs elaborated. "They're being held in cages in the back. My escape plan will require the assistance of Harry and Mingus. And I have a friend on the ground named Shelly. He's a rat who lives in the palace."

"How the hell can we trust a rat?" asked Harry.

"Yeah, rats will eat the eyes out of the dead," Teak added.

"I'll vouch for Shelly. He knows all about Lindsey's work in DC. He's on our side."

Harry nodded. He seemed to trust Doctor Biggs, and Teak agreed as well.

Doctor Biggs went on to explain the spring-loaded pin latches, and how Harry and Mingus would have to lift and twist them to open Mom and Dad's cages. They would be in harm's way while they did so because four Taliban soldiers were posted near the kennel, two outside and two inside. Harry and Mingus would enter and exit through a first-story window, two rooms down from the kennel.

It all sounded plausible.

Biggs went on to explain how the Taliban were going to use Ripper and the Old Man to detonate nuclear missiles in America, creating a nuclear holocaust, Bin Laden-style.

My chest grew tight, and I couldn't take a deep breath. I growled as I listened. America would be lost forever over the Old Man's mistake and Ripper's need for power. This changes everything, I thought to myself. I'll have to tell John and Nancy. If there ever was a reason to break the language golden-rule, it was this. We needed to leave as soon as possible for Islamabad.

Teak turned on the TV in the great room and flipped to a local news channel. Doctor Biggs shared that the Old Man's regime had used a drone strike to kill an Afghan family and then lied, claiming they'd killed ISIS-K plotters. Seven children had been killed. I looked at pictures of the dead children on the TV screen and recognized Mojeeb, a kind young boy who was little Michael's friend. How could this be happening, I asked myself, then realized if this could happen, the Old Man and Ripper could nuke America as Taliban patsies.

"Mojeeb was such a sweet little boy. The Old Man is horrific," said Liza.

"Everything the Old Man touches turns to crap," I said, crying for Mojeeb and his family, and wondering what might happen next.

Our troops dispersed, heading to their favorite spots to sleep. It was after two in the morning.

"What does not destroy us makes us stronger," Teak said in a joking manner and added, "Goodnight!"

"Nietzsche never faced Taliban with US M4 carbines and night-vision goggles," Simone replied, and joined Harry on the leather sofa.

Doctor Biggs turned off the TV and reminded us to get some rest. He headed upstairs, flapped his wings, and flew out the window. I watched for a long moment until he disappeared into the night sky.

My dad was a very wise dog who came from a long, illustrious line of famous Mastiffs, who'd guarded great and wise human leaders as well as tyrants of the worst kind; men with power who'd blossomed into their own species of Hitler and Stalin. Taliban leaders wanted him to guard the Presidential Palace. I knew he'd figure a way out, but we didn't have time. Now that we knew Ripper had been set up to betray America, we had to get to Islamabad as soon as possible. Doctor Biggs has a good plan to free Mom and Dad, I told myself, and said a prayer that God would give us the power to do his will and free them.

Catching up with Liza, we cuddled under our favorite tree, gazing at a canopy of stars.

"*Brave New World* and *1984* are two very similar tragedies. Why do humans read them?" asked Liza.

I knew she was trying to distract my attention from worrying about tomorrow night.

"Aldous Huxley thought that humankind would submit to totalitarian rule under mass hypnosis and a drug called Soma," I said, looking into Liza's curious eyes. "George Orwell thought totalitarian rule would arise from a brutal regime that controlled the meaning of language and therefore thoughts and internal freedom, controlling what one is and what one can become. They both feared that humans would be turned into soulless automatons who'd forget the meaning of love and freedom. Huxley thought it would be easier to make people love their servitude, while Orwell thought beating people into submission under the rule of a brutal law would be more practical. The Old Man's regime is like Huxley and Orwell. Who do you think is more effective: the Old Man or the Taliban?"

"I don't want to think about it. It creates a dark phenomenology of now-not-yet affecting what I am and what I might become."

I wagged my tail. "Liza, you're very wise."

"Blue, if the Taliban capture and cage us, will they be able to make us forget about our love for one another?"

"Not in a million years. We have God. He's outside the reach of all material faculties, so they can't take God away. We'll always have the ability to direct our attention to God even at the very end, and our love springs from God, our meaning, and our internal freedom. We'll always have our love."

"I feel so secure in your presence, Blue," Liza said, and snuggled up to me.

"As I do with you, Liza," I replied, and kissed her nose.

"I've been thinking about dolphins," Liza said softly. "Lindsey, the mouse in the White House, uses them to send messages across the Atlantic Ocean. They have a very unique and objective way of communicating which involves echolocation and sonar."

A lightbulb went off in my head. My face lit up with a big smile. Humans could become like land-roving dolphins. That would solve their language-thinking power struggles.

"Liza, that's the most brilliant observation I've ever heard," I said, and licked her face. She was the love of my life; I'd known that in my Sentio since the day Nancy and Kim brought her home. She was my Sentiomate.

"Tell me more about your dad," she said, closing her eyes and nuzzling her head beneath my front paw.

"When Dad was growing up in the monastery, he learned from meditating while watching ripples on a pond spread over the surface, thinking about how love, freedom, knowledge, truth, and meaning spread over the surface of the world. He studied the three wills: Power, Pleasure, and Meaning, and he fasted for three days while studying. Then he directed his attention toward God for two more days before eating."

Liza had fallen asleep. I turned my eyes to the North Star and watched as many other stars emerged beyond.

Thinking about Mom and Dad and when I was a pup, I imagined being free with Liza and them in America. I said another prayer that I'd stop Ripper and the Old Man and fell asleep.

12

Around six-thirty in the evening on August 30, we headed for the Presidential Palace. Few people walked on the streets of Kabul, where Taliban soldiers were posted every block. The women who did wore black and blue burqas, and a few wore hijabs. The men no longer wore jeans. They wore tunics and robes and dark turbans, and most of the men carried long guns. Taliban had changed Afghanistan overnight with their power grab, using Sharia law like Progressive Socialists in the US had used "racism" to change America overnight.

We'd split up into three groups to avoid being noticed. I led Harry, Mingus, and Duke down a row of parallel-parked cars on a side street, zigzagging back and forth from the sidewalk to the street using the cars for cover as we passed through Taliban checkpoints.

Liza, along with Colonel limping on his left leg, Tiny, and Simone followed one block behind. Molly, George, and Teak brought up the rear two blocks back. Doctor Biggs soared overhead, directing us to the palace. Earlier, before we left Number 9, Biggs informed me that he'd met with Shelly, and they'd choreographed the liberation of Rae and BB. Biggs also briefed Harry and Mingus, who'd volunteered to free Mom and Dad, which was a wonderful act of strange love.

The palace rose up on the horizon like the horn of a unicorn. There was a turret tower in the middle and concrete buildings with flying buttresses on each side. There were no windows. I noticed a Taliban checkpoint in front. It would be impossible to gain access to the palace via that entrance. Harry, Mingus, Duke, and I waited behind a tree about two hundred yards from the palace gate. Liza, Colonel, Tiny, and Simone arrived and hid behind another tree. Molly, George, and Teak waited beside a parked car on the street.

Around eight in the evening, Doctor Biggs came flying back to us, gliding low on his three-foot wing span and carrying Shelly in his talons. Harry, Mingus, Duke, and I gathered round and introduced ourselves to Shelly.

Shelly greeted us and wasted no time. "The Taliban and ISIS are only happy when they can terrorize and hear squeals from their prisoners. They love to torture and decapitate loved ones in front of one another. So, Mingus and Harry, you must do exactly as I say."

Shelly was a bold little rat who didn't mince his words. I liked him. He spoke the truth, and we all knew the stakes. Harry and Mingus looked nervous as they turned cautiously and followed Shelly toward the west side of the palace. Doctor Biggs flapped his wings and said, "I'll be overhead watching. Everyone else stays put. We'll leave for Bagram from here when BB and Rae are free."

I barked softly in support and wished him Godspeed. I really liked Doctor Biggs. He was a great part of our family, and he gave us air reconnaissance superiority.

About thirty minutes later, Doctor Biggs landed near our tree, looking frustrated.

"What's wrong?" I asked.

"Those damn night vision goggles. The two Taliban guards outside are wearing them. We're going to need to create a diversion for BB and Rae's escape."

My mind raced. "What kind of diversion?"

Colonel had joined us. "Doctor Biggs, how about Tiny, George, and Duke fake a fight?"

"That could work," said Biggs, rotating his head toward Duke.

Colonel gathered the Great Dane, Rottweiler, and German Shepherd and explained the plan. They all smiled and, in unison, said, "Let's go start a dogfight."

The three dogs would "fight," making a lot of noise while not hurting one another, giving bloodcurdling roars and foaming at the mouth. They were to start fighting on Doctor Bigg's signal, which was three hoots. I'd scout on the ground watching for surprises while the dogs fought, and then I'd lead the retreat once Mom and Dad were free.

Doctor Biggs wanted to use the east side for the distraction to draw the guards from the escape window. So off we went, with me leading the way around the east lawn of the palace, following a wide path toward the back with Doctor Biggs scouting high above.

13

Back in Washington, DC, Lindsey the white-footed mouse had been to the kitchen, eating scraps from the Old Man's lunch table. Today he'd feasted on lobster and filet mignon. He was returning to his quarters with a full belly and ready for a nap in the Presidential Suite when he saw lights on in the Situation Room. The squeaks of chairs indicated lots of people were in attendance. He figured something big was being discussed.

He headed back into the wall and climbed to the ceiling, then scurried along the electrical cable to the center light fixture. The Old Man's military team donned their red and black uniforms. Roani wore a yellow dress, and Horrid wore a white and black dress, making her resemble a Holstein cow. Suki wore a purple suit matching her hair. Lindsey almost vomited after eyeing the group's attire.

Kline, Sallivan, Koby, Roani, Blank, Horrid, Suki, McCow, Austere, and Ripper sat around the oblong cherry table in the Situation Room.

Roani explained that COVID will be far better than nuclear weapons once we learn how to manipulate medical science, and added, "China uses COVID as a weapon to evoke fear in their peasants, turning them into herds, more easily controlled."

Blank and Koby chuckled.

"General Ripper, have you received your third shot?" asked Roani with a smirk on her face.

"My essence comes from my potency. Do you think I'd risk developing COVID impotency?"

"What do you mean?" asked Roani.

"Of course I got my third and fourth boosters."

"Okay, let's get started, shall we," Roani said, giving a nod to Ripper.

"General Austere and General McCow, you're both familiar with our No-Horizon No-Recall Nuclear retaliation package," Ripper said. "For those who don't know, we've developed the most robust program ever envisioned to prevent a first strike or lone-wolf nuclear strike on America. We have fifty long-range ICBM missiles aimed at our greatest enemies around the world. No-Horizon allows us to launch all fifty missiles with the push of one button, and once activated, that signal can never be recalled. So if Russia or China threaten our Old Man, they know they're one button away from global thermonuclear war."

Horrid cackled like a hyena.

Suki blew a large bubble-gum bubble; it popped, covering her face.

Austere buried his face in his hands.

"General Ripper, surely there has to be a way to recall such an attack if made by mistake," said Admiral Koby.

"No, sir, the beauty of this is deterrence. We'll never have to push the button."

"But General Ripper, what if the button is pushed by accident?" asked Roani.

"Accidents are unacceptable," replied Ripper.

"But General, accidents happen," Kline said. "We have an Old Man running the push button switch."

Ripper sighed, appearing frustrated. "We'll have twenty minutes to scramble our Air Force to destroy the missiles in their silos."

"General, that's not enough time," Roani said. "We won't have enough time to get our families to safety in the underground shelter in West Virginia."

"I meant thirty minutes. My bad," said Ripper.

"Won't that destroy America?" asked Blank.

"Yes, America as we know it will be destroyed, but our government will thrive underground. And the rest of the world will be eternally grateful," Ripper said. "The Old Man has already approved No-Horizon. I wanted everyone familiar with the plan and lingo. We need mainstream media promoting this package."

Lindsey ran along the cable and up to the roof. He'd never heard such nonsense before. No-Horizon sounded insane. Why would Ripper promote such a disaster waiting to happen? There could only be one reason. Ripper wanted to assist the Old Man in accidentally destroying America.

He had to get the information to animals in Kabul. He wanted to make sure No-Horizon had nothing to do with Afghanistan and the Taliban.

Lindsey whistled for Edith, who was eating bread crumbs on the South Lawn. She flew up top, listened carefully, and then flew toward the Atlantic Coast.

14

"I'll free BB, and you free Rae," Mingus said, looking at Harry beneath the open window in the back of the palace.

"No one goes in till I give the order," Shelly said. "I'll be right back."

Shelly ran to the tree where Doctor Biggs had landed.

"Do we have a diversion for our escape?" asked Shelly.

"Yes. When BB and Rae are free and at the window, Tiny, Duke, and George are going to fake a fight on the opposite side of the palace, drawing attention away from that window."

"I'm going in with Harry and Mingus. I know the palace inside and out."

Doctor Biggs flapped his wings. "Godspeed."

Shelly climbed through the window first, jumped to the beige marble floor, then whispered for Harry and Mingus to follow. Shelly peeked down the canary yellow hall. Two Taliban soldiers wearing black turbans and red robes marched back and forth in their US military boots, four doors down, toting M4 carbines.

"We're going to need a distraction," Shelly murmured to Harry and Mingus.

"What do you mean?" asked Harry.

"I mean, we'll never get into the kennel with those soldiers guarding just outside."

Harry took a look down the hallway. "How about a little game of cat and mouse?"

Shelly smiled. "That could work. I'll run down the hall with Mingus chasing me. There's a kitchen at the end of the hall. We can hide in the cabinets or under the table or sink; there are lots of options."

Mingus grinned like a Cheshire cat.

"I'll wait till the soldiers chase you, then I'll free BB and Rae," said Harry.

"Mingus, we'll wait till we hear the dogs barking outside, then we'll double back," said Shelly.

Mingus gave a nod to Shelly.

"Everybody get ready," Shelly said. "When I run, Mingus count to two and then chase me."

"We're ready," said Harry.

"Let's roll." Shelly shot down the hallway like a bullet. Mingus counted then sprinted after him. Shelly figured the guards wouldn't shoot because they'd disturb Harkoni and Badass.

One soldier tried to hit Shelly with the butt of his gun. The other fell trying to stomp on him, tripping on the laces of his US Army boots.

Harry watched, holding back laughter as the soldiers dropped their guns and pursued Mingus and Shelly into the kitchen. Harry made his move down the hall and was inside the kennel in a second.

"Harry, thank God. Get Rae out first. We've had no food or water for the last twenty-four hours," said BB.

"No Paws Left Behind. We've got you both covered," Harry said as he freed Rae.

She stepped onto the marble floor and stretched for a long moment. "God bless you, Harry."

BB was freed next, and he stretched and looked down the hallway toward the sounds of pots and pans striking the floor.

Harry hurried BB and Rae to the escape window two doors down on the right. BB raised his head, and Doctor Biggs produced three hoots.

Tiny, Duke, and George began fighting and barking. George let out a ferocious roar. The Taliban soldiers outside ran toward their diversion.

BB looked at Rae, then Harry.

"Don't worry. They're creating a distraction. Let's go out the window and hide in the trees to the left," said Harry.

Rae went first. Harry followed, and BB hit the ground running. Doctor Biggs joined them. BB and Rae thanked him, and BB explained that they couldn't go back to Number 9 because the Taliban would search there first. They'd need to rest tonight and leave for Islamabad tomorrow night. Rae was weak and exhausted, and they could eat and sleep in house Number 3.

Doctor Biggs flew off to spread the word. The teams would rendezvous at house Number 3.

Shelly and Mingus ran out of the kitchen with the Taliban soldiers following. Mingus took a quick right and jumped out the window, landing in full gallop. Shelly kept running and made it into his hole in the wall while Tiny, Duke, George, and Blue ran back around to the trees in front of the palace.

15

B ack in house Number 3, Rae and BB filled up on water and dry dog food. Everyone was accounted for but Simone.

"Where is Simone?" Mom asked.

"She was right behind me as we crossed L Street, where the Taliban drove a US Humvee right at us," said Colonel.

"I had to jump up on the curb to avoid the Humvee," said Liza.

Harry cried, "We've got to find her."

I walked over to Harry and reassured him we'd find Simone and bring her home.

Tiny, Duke, George, Mingus, and I headed out the back door. We ran toward L Street, where I picked up Simone's scent and followed it to some debris on the side of the road. There, next to an old mop, Simone's beautiful body lay lifeless, her tan fur bloodstained. I licked her face but got no response. She'd been run over, crushed by a large vehicle, probably the Humvee.

Simone was dead. I cried and grabbed her body by

the nape of her neck. Tiny, Duke, George, and Mingus caught up with me and, with their heads low, trudged behind me, back to house Number 3. I laid Simone down on the patio and went to tell Harry.

Doctor Biggs flew in. He'd stayed to make sure Shelly was okay. I told him about Simone and then walked inside to tell Harry. He already knew. Harry cried and ran to hug Simone.

Liza and Mom cried. Our entire family had lost a wonderful member.

"Simone gave her life for my freedom, Rae's freedom, and our puppies' freedom," said Dad.

I cried some more and cuddled next to Liza in the kitchen. After a couple of hours of mourning, Doctor Biggs gave a eulogy for Simone. George and Duke dug a grave in the backyard, and I lowered Simone's body to its final resting spot. Dad said a beautiful prayer that ended with "someday we'll all be together again," lifting our spirits and giving us hope.

Mom, Dad, and Teak continued to console Harry.

Liza and I found a knoll in the backyard and cuddled under the moon, feeling sad that Harry didn't have Simone but happy that we had each other.

"What is God?" Liza asked in a soft voice.

"That's a tough question; that's very personal."

"Your dad's prayer was wonderful."

"Thank you," I said, and considered how to best answer her question. "My dad explains God this way. God is the unique source of all that is good in the world. God is beyond the reach of all our material faculties, but we have the capacity to direct our attention toward God and channel goodness into the world. God is also key in maintaining internal freedom, love, and meaning under extreme conditions like at Auschwitz and Dachau, where everything that was within reach of one's material faculties was taken away by soldiers of tyranny. They marched human attention into ruts, which became prison walls for nonbelievers. It's like what the Progressive Socialists are trying to achieve in America and what the Taliban have achieved in Afghanistan. In the end, God is goodness."

"Everyone yearns for goodness, Blue. We all yearn for God," Liza replied.

"Yes, but some yearn for power more than goodness. Tomorrow, I'll tell Dad about Ripper and the Old Man's No-Horizon nuclear holocaust and my plan to talk with John and Nancy."

"I think your dad will agree with your plan. You'll both have to sit down and have a long talk with John and Nancy about Ripper and the Old Man."

"We must get to Islamabad as soon as possible," I whispered.

Liza nodded and fell asleep with her head on my right paw. I thanked God for her.

Chapter

16

After receiving an update from Lindsey, Doctor Biggs had a long talk with Dad the next day about the Taliban's plot to use Ripper to trick the Old Man and then destroy America with their own nuclear weapons—Bin Laden-style.

Dad wasn't convinced that such a thing as No-Horizon would ever be approved in the US. I approached Biggs and Dad in the kitchen of house Number 3.

"But Dad, we can't take that chance. Lindsey reported that Ripper said No-Horizon had already been approved by the Old Man, and Shelly reported that the Taliban acknowledged No-Horizon's existence."

"Blue, let me think about this. It makes no sense. We need more evidence."

"The Old Man and Ripper hate America. There's your evidence. That makes sense."

"Don't let your bad feelings distort you, son. Thou shalt not bear false witness against thy neighbor."

I shook my head and turned away. I couldn't believe

what my dad had said, and then he'd recited the Ninth Commandment. I knew he was right that we had no tangible evidence. After a long moment, I turned around and apologized. Dad was always calm and wise. He was Wise One. I agreed that I had bad feelings toward the Old Man and Ripper and that I'd reassess things after my bad feelings cleared. Usually, over time, by redirecting my attention away from a subject like the Old Man and Ripper, my bad feelings toward them would clear. I'd have to wait till I could think objectively about all the evidence. The Progressive Socialists had used a hoax to destroy their former president, and I didn't want to be a part of anything like that.

We all filled up on food and water, and at sunset, we began our long journey. We split up into three groups, and Doctor Biggs flew ahead. Harry led my group, which also had Mom and Dad. Mingus led Duke, George, and Tiny in Group Two. Molly led Liza, Teak, and Colonel in Group Three. The cats led because they had better night vision.

We headed for Bagram, walking along a dark highway. I walked next to Dad, thinking about life and meaning. I still hadn't figured out the grand meaning of life, the seven-dimensional jigsaw puzzle. I wondered about the meaning of Simone's life.

"Dad, what's the grand meaning of life? I'm having a hard time right now."

"Don't be so hard on yourself," Dad said, and nudged me with his nose.

"I feel like I'm running out of time. What was the meaning of Simone's life?"

"Simone gave her life for my freedom, Rae's freedom, and our puppies' freedom. She'd maintained her internal freedom and connection with God. Then she made the ultimate sacrifice, giving strange love to Rae and me, and our puppies. That was her meaning. She knew it too," Dad said, and turned, encouraging Mom to hold his tail in her mouth as we climbed another hill.

Dad pulled Mom as I reflected about Simone. She had been a wonderful being, and she'd wanted to free Mom and Dad despite the risks. I nudged Dad with my nose. "Tell me about meaning."

"The will for meaning in individuals is an odyssey for freedom: freedom from slavery and from tyranny," Dad explained. "It starts and ends with internal freedom of attention, which requires God. It culminates in freedom from the misery of need and the bondage of time, experiencing the ecstasy of infinity in the presence of goodness and God. We fulfill our meaning out of love for one another. Love comes from God, who loved us first."

"That's the most beautiful explication of meaning I've ever heard."

"Thank you, Blue. Meaning is personal, or it doesn't fulfill the individual. In America, Fraudra's meaning cannot be forced on others to fulfill, for example," Dad said, and rubbed against my shoulder.

I'd heard about Fraudra, the congresswoman from New York City, and her power grab. Americans were not stupid. I knew that from John and Nancy. They'd never adopt institutional or political meaning.

"Institutional meaning doesn't work," I said.

"Exactly, and to find meaning, one must have the ability to direct one's attention to one's rich life experiences and God, especially under extreme conditions," Dad replied.

"Like what we are going through now."

"Yes," Dad said as we reached the top of the hill. Mom released his tail, and Dad shot her a smile.

"Remember our discussion about meaning under the pistachio tree when I was a pup? You gave me a complex puzzle to figure out. I haven't figured it out yet," I said, picking up the pace down a gravel road, trying to keep up with Harry and Dad.

Dad slowed and acknowledged that he remembered our discussion about meaning. "If you follow the will for the meaning of individuals into the future toward infinity, their meanings will become one. We're all on this journey that will culminate in freedom from the misery of need and from the bondage of time—freedoms inconceivable and unachievable without internal freedom, love, and God. The grand meaning is to reach out and touch the hand of God and dwell in the presence of goodness," Dad said, and looked back to check on Mom.

"So that's the mystery," I said in amazement. "Love and freedom drive our divergent meanings, which become one as we approach infinity, trying to obtain freedom from the misery of need and bondage of time. Internal freedom, love, and God are our destiny, our purpose. That's my meaning."

"Yes. If you maintain internal freedom, give love, and pursue God, you'll fulfill your meaning. Internal freedom is key. Addiction to drugs, power, money, food, etcetera, take away your internal freedom by driving your attention and phenomenology to feed your addiction."

The power-addicted American Progressive Socialists were perfect examples of what Dad was saying.

Everything they did was a calculation for what would deliver them more power.

Pursuing God requires internal freedom and love. Mom and Dad had given me both. I directed my attention to God, and in prayer, I asked for God to open a channel to allow goodness and love to flow into the world through me to fulfill my meaning.

A sign up ahead read ten kilometers to Nuristan Mountain Forest. The first light of dawn broke, and we needed to find food and water and a place to sleep. I ran ahead and found a stream of blue-green water with a cozy bank of green moss hidden from sight by a small group of trees. It was perfect for our troop. I signaled to Doctor Biggs, and he flew off to tell the other two groups.

In the meantime, Harry had caught a rabbit-like creature, a lagomorph, and two birds. He dropped them off, and I followed him. We caught two more lagomorphs; they were everywhere. Duke and George chomped on a bird and complained it tasted like chicken. Tiny enjoyed a lagomorph feast, then he chewed on a tree root. I gave a tree root a try, and it was pretty good. Colonel ate roots and grass. He still didn't look well.

The sun rose and warmed our camp. Dad and Mom took a long drink at the stream and fell asleep together on the moss shaded by tree branches. Liza and I shared some meat and settled by the stream. Mingus caught a fish and shared it with Molly. Teak and Harry, once adversaries as DLM and CLM members, now worked together like brothers. Sleeping lightly, they maintained guard duty under a tree overlooking the stream bank, and Doctor Biggs roosted on a branch high above them.

17

In the spartan US Embassy Compound in Islamabad, standing in the kitchen of a small apartment designed for Marines, Nancy Blair stood over a stove, wearing a blue dress and green apron and stirring a pot of beans. She and her family had been evacuated from Kabul and were waiting for reassignment. She picked up her iPhone and redialed Asha, her housekeeper in Kabul. She'd been trying to reach her for the last three weeks.

"Hello?"

"Asha, is that you?"

"Mrs. Blair," Asha replied, crying into the phone.

"Thank God. Are you okay?"

"No, I'm not okay. I'm not okay. They beheaded Dari." She cried louder. "I escaped and am trying to get to Iran."

"God help us!" Nancy cried. "I'm so sorry. God bless you."

"Dari and I had to leave the animals. The Taliban marked your house."

"Oh, I'm so heartbroken. We are so sad. Michael

and Kim have cried themselves to sleep every night for Rae, BB, Blue, and Liza. I don't know what to do."

"I'm so sorry for the children. I love them, Rae, BB, and the others. I've been crying too. The animals are probably dead. The Taliban had US weapons and ammo, and they shot and killed everything on K Street. America's Old Man has helped destroy his own people and animals, and he killed little Mojeeb and his family with a drone strike."

"I know this has been a horrific situation for so many. I can't tell the children about Dari, Mojeeb, or the animals," Nancy said, her voice trembling and tears streaming down her cheeks.

Michael, a cute little seven-year-old with large brown eyes and brown hair, walked into the kitchen. He felt the urge to cry after seeing his mother's tears. "What's wrong?" he asked, and hugged his mom around the waist.

Nancy ran her fingers through his hair and hugged his neck. "Asha, I've got to go. We are going to help you," Nancy said. "John will help you. Call me tomorrow night."

Kim, a precocious thirteen-year-old with golden locks, came skipping into the kitchen. "What's wrong?"

Nancy ended her call. "Nothing. I'm just upset."

"Tell us. That was Asha," said Michael.

"I don't want to talk now, sweetheart."

"Are they okay? Rae, BB, Blue, and Liza, are they, Mother?" asked Kim.

Nancy shook her head.

"America's Old Man has destroyed our lives," Kim said, crying. "You and Dad voted for him. How could you?"

Michael cried, and Nancy crouched and hugged him. "They're not dead," Michael cried. "Blue will find us, and he'll lead the others to us. I know he will."

Kim hugged her mother and brother. They all sobbed for several long moments, then three knocks on the door rang out.

"It's going to be okay," Nancy said, and kissed Michael and Kim.

Michael rubbed his eyes. "They'll find us. I know they will."

"What can we do?" asked Kim.

"I'll talk to your dad tonight. We're going to do everything we can," Nancy said, taking off her apron and then hurrying to the door.

Michael hugged his sister and told her not to worry. He knew Blue would find a way to freedom. "Blue and I have a secret. I can't tell anyone because I promised. But he's really smart, and he'll find us."

Kim smiled through her tears and wrapped her arms around Michael again. "I hope Rae and her puppies are okay. I hate America's Old Man and his lame regime."

"Sis, I know. Dad says you shouldn't hate, though. It will be okay. Dad will stop the Old Man, or when I grow up, I'll stop him."

18

We'd been traveling through the Nuristan Mountain Forest for the last twelve days, relying on the kindness of strangers, as Simone had suggested. Kind Afghan mountain people had provided us with lentils, bread, and meat several times over the last week.

Snow-capped mountains, V-shaped valleys, and rugged stone mountain slopes decorated the terrain. Small streams and patches of green grass with groups of trees, mostly cedar pines, had provided us a safe haven for several long, windy nights. We'd decided to travel by day because of all the unknowns and danger we knew were lurking out there. We'd met a pack of wild dogs who were hungry, scrounging for food, a couple of days ago. They'd barked at Harry and Mingus until Teak stepped up and talked them down.

The dogs warned us about a wolf pack with a killer alpha wolf who'd murdered two of their members. Dad and Mom seemed very concerned. I was concerned for Harry, Mingus, Molly, and Teak because they couldn't defend themselves against wolves.

Doctor Biggs had left three days ago, traveling back to Kabul to get more evidence against Ripper and the Old Man. Dad had reconsidered my concern and sent Biggs to the Presidential Palace for more data.

I'd been thinking a lot over the last two days. I'd figured out my meaning. I had to talk to John and Nancy and warn them about Ripper and the Old Man's nuclear holocaust.

As we made it around another bend in the trail, following the river toward Pakistan, I walked faster and caught up with Dad.

"Dad, I'm no longer having bad feelings. I've looked at the evidence objectively. The Old Man has demonstrated to us what he is capable of doing. Just consider the drone strike that killed Mojeeb. I have to talk to John and Nancy—"

"Blue!" Dad whispered as loud as he could, interrupting me. "Rae spotted a wolf. Everyone stays calm. Spread the word. No one runs, no matter what."

Our troop gathered around Dad and Mom, everyone looking over their shoulders. My heart was pounding, and I was ready to fight.

"Molly and Mingus, I want you to walk with me and BB. Harry and Teak walk with Tiny, George, and Duke. Blue, Colonel, and Liza, you'll bring up the rear," said Mom.

I looked ahead and saw a single large tree about two hundred yards away. Harry, Mingus, and Molly could climb the tree. I told Mom and Dad.

"We see the tree. Watch Liza and Colonel's backs," said Mom.

Then, out of nowhere, a large gray wolf appeared on the rocky mountain slope to our left. I barked to get everyone's attention. There had to be fifteen wolves approaching. They were walking fast, but not running, like they were toying with us.

Four wolves and the alpha wolf approached Mom and Dad. Mom picked up her pace, shielding Mingus and Molly. Dad slowed down, and I could see the hair standing up on his neck. He turned and charged the alpha wolf, who yelped and backed down.

The four wolves surrounded Dad and snapped at him from all sides. He let out a thunderous roar that shook the ground beneath my feet. He slung two wolves to the ground with his powerful paws. I'd never seen him so angry, and I knew he would fight to the death protecting Mom and her puppies. George the Rott-weiler, with super strong jaws, ran to help. He and Dad got a wolf on the ground, and George bit him hard, breaking his hind leg. I'd heard it snap. The wolves limped away and licked their wounds.

Just when I thought they'd left, five more wolves approached Colonel, Liza, and me. I stood on my hind legs and let out a roar. Three wolves went after Colonel, who still had a limp from his wounded left leg and could barely fend off one wolf. I pounced on the third wolf who was savagely attacking Colonel, and he turned and bit my shoulder, drawing blood. A sharp pain went through my neck, creating rage in me.

Suddenly I was stronger than I'd ever been before. I grabbed the wolf by the throat, slinging him to and fro, crushing his trachea and killing him, but not before he bit my leg. Damn, their teeth were sharp. Liza, the love of my life, was under attack. I ran to her side growling ferociously and jumped on the two wolves near her, biting them both on the neck, resulting in their retreat.

The two wolves remaining who'd attacked us scattered. Colonel was down. They'd bitten completely through his left leg, tearing it to shreds.

I turned my eyes toward Mom and Dad and saw that Mingus and Molly were climbing the tree, and Harry had Teak by the nape of his neck and was pulling him up the tree to safety. Liza and I stayed where we were and guarded Colonel.

After making sure the cats were safe, Dad, Duke, Tiny, and George came running to help us. There must have been ten wolves surrounding us, growling and showing their teeth. They were closing in, stalking in a tighter and tighter pattern, jaws open and slavering, eyes gleaming as they anticipated the kills to come.

Dad let out a roar and came charging in, swatting two wolves into the air with his massive paws. When they hit the ground, George, Duke, and Tiny were all over them, growling and biting them violently. I ran toward the alpha wolf, and he took off toward the mountain. The wolf pack retreated up the mountain slope.

I dragged Colonel by the neck as we made our way to the tree by the calm green stream. Mother tended to his wounds; he was in bad shape. I glanced back and noticed several wolves had returned to our battlefield and were tearing the wolf I'd killed apart. Damn those wolves. Liza was still shaking, and my heart pounded.

I gazed into Liza's eyes and licked her nose. "I'm proud of the way you fought."

"Blue, you were awesome," she said, her voice quivering.

Doctor Biggs flew in, returning from his trip to Kabul. "There are about fifteen wolves left in this pack.

I spotted the alpha wolf on a hill a couple of hundred yards down the trail. Looks like they want to trap you in the narrow passageway ahead."

Rae looked at BB. "What are we going to do?"

Dad shook his head, appearing concerned and frustrated. "We'll have to stay here tonight."

Harry and Mingus jumped down from the tree. Mingus went to work licking Colonel's wounds.

Harry glanced at Dad. "Those damn wolves butchered his leg and back, and he looks like crap. I'm going to catch some dinner; hopefully, he'll eat something."

Harry went searching for small game, and Teak came down the tree with Molly and went to work licking Colonel's wounds. Shaking my head in disgust, I approached. I could see his bone within the wound.

I didn't want to eat after looking at those open wounds. I settled next to Liza, Mom, and Dad, lying at the base of the tree, thinking about my bad feelings toward the wolves.

"Dad, what is hate?"

"Hate is the result of victim-thinking. It's that simple," Dad said tersely. "The infamous tyrants like Hitler and Stalin used hate to control and manipulate the masses, and we know that hate makes people less objective and incapable of love, and also incapable of finding the truth. Remember when your mother and I scolded you for criticizing the Old Man?"

I turned my eyes toward Mom. "Yes."

"We did that to prevent you from developing victim-thinking and the phenomenology of hate," said Mom.

"What about the hate I feel for the wolves?"

"That's survival; it's not hate. It's your will to live,

engaging every ounce of your strength to survive," said Dad.

"Is it like the will for power?"

"Yes, in a strange way, it is connected to the will for power," Dad said. "But not the will for power the Progressive Socialists are driven by in their attempt to control America. That's a pathological will for power, like a drug addiction. Everything they do is consumed by their need for power. Your will to live is a good thing."

Harry had found some small game, wild pheasants, and Mom, Dad, Liza, and the others shared. Colonel nibbled on a bird but didn't eat more than a bite.

We tried to sleep, but I couldn't rest. The wolves seemed to howl, harass us, and instill fear, like the Taliban shot US M4 carbines into the night sky. Every time I drifted toward sleep, they'd wake me up.

By morning I wanted to take on the alpha wolf. I thought that if we could kill him, the pack would disperse, and we could go on our way. If Dad and the others could hold off the wolf pack, I knew I was fast enough to catch the alpha wolf. I was taller and heavier than him too, but he had razor-sharp teeth. I knew it would be dangerous, my life on the line for our freedom. That thought seemed to give me strength. My body rejuvenated at the opportunity to win our freedom.

As the sun rose, I discussed my plan to take on the alpha male with Mom and Dad.

"If we do this, I'm going to break away from our camp, and I'll have your back, keeping the alpha wolf's guards at bay while Tiny, Duke, and George keep the other wolves occupied," said Dad.

"I'm afraid," said Mom.

I nudged Mother with my nose and licked her face. "I've got to do this."

Liza had been listening. "I'm going to break away too. I'll have your back, Blue."

19

I'd spent my life wrestling with Dad, who was the strongest dog I'd ever known. I was quicker than him, and I'd learned to take his punches and bites. I just wanted one chance to take the alpha male down. I'd grab his throat and suffocate him. But first, I'd need to stop him from turning and grabbing me with his wickedly sharp teeth. I'd need to get on top of him, I told myself, and sink my teeth around the front part of his neck.

Around sundown, the wolves made their move. The pack formed an arc around our tree by the stream. Mingus, Molly, Harry, and Teak were safe in the tree. Duke, George, Tiny, Liza, Rae, BB, and I held our ground, protecting Colonel. Doctor Biggs scouted overhead.

The wolves attacked, and we fought them off. They were sneaky, though. They tried multiple strategies to penetrate and overload our wall of defense to get at Colonel. I didn't let that happen. I fought them off two at a time from the right flank. Dad and George were on the left side of our defense, and soon they killed another wolf by trapping him in the stream and drowning him.

The alpha wolf walked quickly, moving away from our wall of defense, then reversed, and ran full speed right at us as the other wolves moved deliberately in for the kill. I broke ranks and went after the alpha wolf, knocking him down the sloped ground, and we both rolled into the grass. He got up facing me and growled, showing his nostrils and four super large canine teeth. I could see rage rising up in his eyes. His two guard wolves approached and snapped at my legs. I ignored them and kept my focus on my target.

Liza and Dad barked ferociously at the two guard wolves and held them off while George, Tiny, Duke, and Mom kept the other wolves at bay. It was just the alpha male and me. I growled, showing my side teeth, and approached the killer wolf with caution. He lunged at me, trying to bite my right leg. I raised up in reflex, and he backed up. Then he attacked my leg again. I jumped forward, mounted his back, and turned my body around, leaning in with all my weight to push him to the ground so he couldn't break free.

He turned his head and tried to bite me, and I took advantage. Moving lightning fast, I sunk my teeth into his neck. I had him, and I wouldn't let go. He twisted and squirmed with everything he had. I bit hard, then harder, and flipped him on his back, keeping my jaws clenched around his neck. I felt life leaving this creature. I crunched his trachea and released him. He rolled over, hobbled a few feet, and collapsed. The wolf pack watched, bewildered. Their leader was dead. Dad, George, and Duke chased after the wolves as they turned and ran off into the night.

Liza came to my side and licked my right shoulder and leg, which were bleeding. The alpha male had bitten me twice, and my adrenaline surge had blocked my awareness. I was exhausted. I walked slowly back to the tree where Colonel was dying.

"BB, tell Conan I love him. Please get the message to him," Colonel said, his voice trembling.

Doctor Biggs looked on. "I'll make sure."

Dad held his paw as life left his body. We watched for several minutes. Mom licked his nose. Colonel was dead.

Mingus, Teak, Harry, and Molly came down from the tree. We all gathered around and cried.

"He led me to free all of our troop on that pivotal night on K Street. I'll never forget him," I said.

Tiny and Duke dug a hole by the stream. I dragged Colonel's body to its final resting place. Dad said a prayer, and Doctor Biggs reminded us of Colonel's love for Conan and his sacrifices for our freedom.

We covered his grave with rocks and headed out in darkness so that we could get through the narrow passage while the wolves were in disarray. We walked with heavy hearts, our heads hanging low. Liza and I brought up the rear.

"Conan's father was a great man. He loved us too, and he didn't like the Progressive Socialists calling him a racist for his work in the military," said Liza.

I walked slowly. "The racist argument is a fake power argument," I explained. "The only legitimate argument about race is what makes us equal. And one cannot be more equal than others. We all have the ability to direct our attention toward God and the capacity to channel goodness into the world. When we all commit to 'No Paws Left Behind,' we're all equal."

Liza nudged me with her nose and licked my face. "Blue, I love you so much. I knew you would defeat the alpha wolf, but I was still frightened that I might lose you."

"I love you," I said as my eyes filled with tears. "We will always be together. If one of us lives, we both live."

Liza rubbed up against me, her face glowing, as we walked through the narrow passageway, guarded on both sides by mountain slopes and jagged rocks. We'd walked into and out of the valley of the shadow of death.

Chapter

20

The next day, we awoke late in the morning and lay on the soft grass, warming in the sun as Doctor Biggs explained what he'd discovered in Kabul. He'd found incriminating evidence from Shelly. Harkoni and Badass had extorted ten billion dollars from General Ripper and the Old Man. That would never have happened without dirt on Ripper. Shelly figured the Taliban would go for more money and build their wealth before destroying America with a nuclear holocaust.

Doctor Biggs went on to say that Lindsey from the White House had heard directly from Ripper and Roani that even if the Old Man accidentally destroyed America with a nuclear holocaust, he would not face consequences. They can't impeach him or try him for a crime because Progressive Socialists in congress will protect him. Hearing that sent chills down my spine. If the Old Man and the Progressive Socialists don't like America, they can destroy it with no consequences. I lowered my head and said a prayer—God help America.

"Blue, you were right. Now we have evidence," Dad said, shaking his head in sadness.

"I didn't want to be right; I just knew it in my Sentio," I said, and raised my chin more determined to stop them.

"You have grown into a wise one."

"Dad, we must stop Ripper and the Old Man's nuclear holocaust."

"We'll sit down with John and Nancy, and for the first time in human history, we'll talk to humans to save the world," Dad said.

My mind lit up in waves of joy. I couldn't believe what I was hearing. Woohoo! I thought to myself. Dad was on board. We had evidence: ten billion dollars. He knew the world was in terrible jeopardy in the hands of the Old Man, the Taliban, and Ripper.

I jumped up, ready to run all the way to Islamabad, but instead walked beside Dad as our troop began another day's march, trekking down a steep, rocky slope and then finding a trail in the Khyber Pass.

We crossed another hill, and Doctor Biggs landed near Dad and Mom, announcing, "We're in Pakistan!"

Duke, George, Tiny, Harry, Mingus, Molly, Liza, Teak, and I let out a cheer that echoed for miles. We'd made it. Peshawar was only a couple of days away. Then in another ten or eleven days, we'd be at our new home with John, Nancy, Kim, and Michael in Islamabad.

After our celebration, all was quiet as we slowly made our way toward a village in the distance. We could get water, food, and rest there. Walking next to Dad, I thought about truth. Hunger and thirst are real, and they drive my attention to a material truth for satisfaction like good food and water. I know these things to be true when I encounter them.

"What is truth?"

Dad looked at me and smiled. "You know my son, in your Sentio."

"Tell me the story of truth," I asked, thinking of all the wonderful stories Dad had told me when I was a pup.

"Well, the story doesn't have a happy ending, but it is satisfying," Dad said, wagging his tail. "Before Aristotle, the truth was what showed itself. Aristotle said the essence of truth is agreement. Truth is the agreement of knowledge with its object. What is knowledge? Knowledge is the immediate projection of sense data into Sentio consciousness. All positive knowledge must come through as experience in Sentio.

"Then Kant said that objects in the world are noumena and those objects appear in our minds as phenomena, different than noumena. Our perception of things in the world is not exactly the same as the way those things exist in the world. Kant's observation was revolutionary and led to a search for an objective basis for all knowledge. That search failed for the most part. Peirce and James came along and advanced the scientific truth, or pragmatic truth, which involves scientists with like minds experimenting and making observations and then arguing with each other over time till the truth emerges. Then Russell tried to create an objective digital world where the world could be reduced to binary numbers and equations."

"So scientific truth is the best. I like the idea of a digital and mathematical truth too. What about COVID?" I asked, furrowing my brow.

"The worldwide COVID explosion that emerged in Wuhan, China, is the best example of how politics corrupts scientific truth. I've never seen greedy politicians kill more people than I have with COVID. The arguments should have remained in university medical arenas and among doctors, clinicians, and researchers all over the world, and not on media talk shows and the halls of the US Congress where the will for power conflicts with scientific truth. The Old Man and his regime lost all objectivity with COVID and our Afghanistan tragedy, and they used a purple-haired lady to spew misinformation."

"Why didn't they let medical professionals treat COVID like other diseases?"

"Blue, they used COVID to direct American attention to build their political phenomenology, their construct to maintain power and control, while the Delta variant surged, killing hundreds of thousands. They should have focused on treatment. They blamed everyone to no avail while they were to blame. They were at fault. The purple head simply stirred up conflict with information that she was given to create a diversion. That was her job."

"She did her job well. I hope she gets what she deserves."

"Blue, you cannot harbor resentment and give love. Forgive this woman and move on. We have bigger things to do now."

I agreed. Dad was right. I forgave the fraud and vowed never to think of her again. We picked up the pace. We made it to the small village, divided into three groups, then made rounds in the open marketplace, relying on the kindness of strangers to give us leftover food: meat, lentils, fish, bread, and water. Harry, Mingus, and Molly hit gold. An older man who wasn't carrying a weapon gave them a bowl of goat's milk.

It was strange seeing men who didn't carry weapons.

Everyone in Afghanistan seemed to have a long gun. Pakistan was different, more civil, relaxed, and welcoming. I liked the vibe. We filled our bellies and found some grass warmed by the sun just outside of town. Our troop fell asleep as Harry and Teak stood guard.

21

E dith and Lindsey talked on the White House roof as General George S. Ripper, Roani, Horrid, and Kline approached the West Wing in full Nazi-CCP regalia.

"I'll bet they're going to the Situation Room," said Lindsey.

"Wonder why they're meeting this late?" asked Edith.

"I need to get down there. It could be something big. I'll see you later." Lindsey ran along the roof, darted into an air vent, and went straight to the center overhead light fixture of the Situation Room.

The Old Man, Ripper, Horrid, Roani, and Kline had taken their seats at the oblong table and were talking about Horrid's recent Mars commercial with child actors, produced to improve her poll numbers.

Horrid cackled as Roani told her she appeared high on shrooms while talking about Mars.

"Goddammit! Can't we prosecute them for saying 'Fuck the Old Man'?" the Old Man said, interrupting Roani.

Horrid cackled louder.

"Sir, it's better to ignore them," said Roani, appearing startled by the Old Man's outburst.

"Don't worry. We'll get the last laugh," said Kline.

"We need to talk about No-Horizon," said Ripper.

"I don't want to talk about deterrence," the Old Man said. "My own citizens hate me."

"They don't hate you. They're racists and not worth our effort," Roani said, and flitted a smile at the Old Man.

"Sir, getting back to No-Horizon ... if we jumped the gun, got a little excited, and pushed the button switch by mistake," Ripper said, and produced an evil grin, "we'd have to destroy those ICBMs and sacrifice America. I want to make that very, very clear."

"I hear, and I agree," Roani said. "Does everyone agree? Everyone?"

Lindsey watched carefully as Kline, Horrid, and the Old Man nodded one after the other.

"America needs to be destroyed and then rebuilt in a couple of hundred years," said the Old Man.

"Progressive leaders have no children or future invested in America," Kline said. "They can live out their lives in luxury underground. Oh, I'm sorry; I forgot about your kids, sir."

"My family will be fine," the Old Man said. "China will help us if it comes to that. What about American survivors? Will they want revenge?"

"Sir, we'll pay them for their losses and invite them to live underground," Kline said. "If they refuse, no worries. Most will die from radiation exposure in less than six weeks. Besides, to the rest of the world, you'll be hailed as a hero for saving them and destroying racist America."

"They deserve it; I despise them. America is nothing but a melting pot for racists, and some are more racist than others," the Old Man said, and farted for several seconds.

Horrid cackled until tears appeared in her eyes.

Lindsey had seen and heard enough. He sprinted over the electrical cable and darted across the ceiling and then shot up a bathroom vent, arriving on the roof. He had to tell Edith. He had to get this new information headed to Afghanistan and around the world as soon as possible, knowing animals would have to step up and expose the Progressive Socialists to save America.

22

My paws thumped on the hard clay, following just behind Dad, as we both digested the latest news Doctor Biggs had delivered from Lindsey in DC. The Old Man wanted to destroy racist America.

"What's the deal with American racists?" I asked, shaking my head about what the Old Man had said.

Dad slowed and met my gaze. "Progressive Socialists are using racism like the Taliban use Sharia law to control and punish their opponents."

"I thought so. America is in trouble. We must stop the Old Man."

"It's not just the Old Man that we'll have to stop," Dad said. "We'll have to stop the Progressive Socialists who are rewriting history proposing the will for racism shaped America. There's no human will for racism. It's a product of a pathologic will for power, and who in America has a pathologic will for power?"

"The Progressive Socialists," I said, and wagged my tail.

Dad grinned. "There are three wills that drive humans—the will for power, pleasure, and meaning. Racism is produced by the will for power gone awry, driving human slavery, Hitler's Master Race theory, and critical race theory, for example. The will for pleasure gone awry drives humans toward debauchery and addiction. The will for meaning has driven humankind toward greater freedom for all and God since the beginning of time. The will for meaning led to the founding of the United States of America, and the only way to beat the will for power gone awry is with a stronger will for meaning. We'll nurture Americans' will for meaning and undermine the Progressive's coup from within by introducing 'No Paws Left Behind' as a catalyst to produce love for one another, just as it has worked for our group."

I smiled at Dad, slowing my pace, thinking how great it'll be when he speaks to humans.

We'd traveled for ten days since leaving Peshawar, and I knew we weren't far from Islamabad. Walking behind Mom and Dad, I noticed Mom's pregnant belly swaying from side to side. For a long moment, I wondered how I would explain this journey to my soon-to-be new brother and sister puppies. Dad slowed and lumbered as he licked Mother's face in encouragement. I thought about how we'd gotten here, all our trials and tribulations, and the deaths of Simone and Colonel. I thought about the events that had led to the fall of Afghanistan and how the Old Man's regime and their politics had put us in harm's way. I thought about all the death and destruction at HKIA, the loss of ninety Afghans mostly women and children, thirteen young men and women Marines, and the beheadings in Kabul like the poor man, Vijay, in house Number 7. Then I thought about the seven children, including Mojeeb, killed by the Old Man's deceptive drone strike. How could this have happened?

"Politics is horrific," I said, and growled with indignation. "It blinds the many because they think they are right. They think their ideas lead to greater freedom and greater meaning, and that's what they've been programmed to believe. Most are made stupid by hate from the propaganda that drives victim thinking. They're trapped as slaves to their political ideology, like puppets. They have no vision for greater freedom for all. They just have an ideological construct that steals their internal freedom."

Dad looked over at me briefly, never breaking stride as he led Mom and our troop down a dirt road. "When humans left nature, they gave up certain freedoms for security," Dad explained. "They entered into an imaginary contract, and in America, that includes life, liberty, and the pursuit of happiness—the best contract of all. The American government has to ensure life, liberty, and the pursuit of happiness under an umbrella for all, underpinned by equality.

"Progressive Socialists in America want to rewrite that contract so only certain things are allowed if those things are for their own good, the good of the few. And who gets to decide? The Progressives do. They want to enslave humankind to their ideas and their meaning under their totalitarian rule. Politics is just a vehicle for them to brainwash their people and crush those who view individual rights as essential for the future of humankind's march toward greater freedom for all."

"What do you mean by brainwash?" I asked, wrinkling my forehead.

Dad stopped for a moment and scratched behind his ear. "Aldous Huxley thought that humans would submit to totalitarian rule under mass hypnosis," Dad said. "Orwell thought totalitarian rule would arise from a brutal regime that controlled the meaning of language and therefore the thoughts and internal freedom of the masses, controlling what they are and what they can become. They were both right.

"Phenomenology is mass hypnosis, and nonstop attention-driving by Socialist media is modern-day Orwellian brutality. They are both forms of brainwashing, erasing one's rich life experiences and replacing them with whatever yields the elitists the most power."

Dad and I picked up the pace. It all made sense. "They use the media to deliver their phenomenology by driving the attention of the masses to their topics and concerns," I said. "They create mental constructs that your attention gets trapped within. All day long, humans reflect on leftist phenomenology, burying their rich life experiences. And the Old Man's regime uses money and government programs like Soma, a drug that results in dependency."

"Very good, Blue," Dad said, and nodded. "And Huxley's mass hypnosis is phenomenology, employed by Socialists to create a perception that delivers them political power. For example, the Old Man and his regime have convinced US citizens that all Americans in Afghanistan who want to leave may leave. They use the US media to reinforce their hypnosis, or phenomenology, by showing pleasant scenes of the Taliban and Afghans.

"But in reality, the Taliban regime has people so frightened they are willing to fall to their deaths clinging to the landing gear of US transport planes rather than face a brutal life under the Taliban's iron fist."

I wagged my tail in agreement as Dad continued, "The Old Man's regime is using both Huxley and Orwell's ideas. However, hypnosis by the mainstream media is not that effective. The media has been exposed as fake, and they also use fake polls as a weapon to accomplish their agenda, pitting one against the opinion of a fake mass of people." Dad paused, shaking his head as if disgusted. "Then they use laws and their corrupt Justice Department to beat dissenters into submission, like Winston was beaten into submission in *1984*. Look at those arrested on Jan 6, 2021, for trespassing. They're still in solitary confinement in DC prisons, dying, while murderers are released without bail. The Progressive Socialists beat their prisoners and drug them, stealing their internal freedom."

I nodded grimly. "They took Winston's internal freedom through imprisonment, drugs, and torture, and he didn't have God. Progressive Socialists have taken God away from Americans, using COVID."

Dad met my eyes, his eyes twinkling with paternal pride. "Yes, very perceptive. There are still some in America seeking the truth, God, and meaning. They see through the Old Man's deception."

"I see through the Old Man's deception."

Dad lowered his chin, looking sad. "The Progressive Socialists have not silenced all their dissenting voices, but they have Social Media behemoths driving attention in their favor. They use Kapo materials, famous comedians, and actors, who post hateful speech about the opposition to undermine internal freedom and God through hate thinking. They post that God does not exist. They suppress opposition voices, and they drive attention to the topics and subject matter they want. Once they capture attention, they win."

"What are Kapo's?" I asked, disgusted by what the Progressives were doing to America.

"They were Jews the Germans used in concentration camps to torture and murder their fellow Jews," Dad replied in a melancholic tone.

"That's horrible. Dad, we must save them. Americans will be killing one another soon." Dad remained silent as my mind raced. Humans were trapped in their language-thinking world driven by hate. We had to free them. Liza's idea about dolphins popped into my head. After several more moments of silence, I met Dad's gaze. "I've been thinking about dolphins. They've directed their attention to sentient consciousness building greater Sentio awareness for millions of years. They've developed a great way to communicate objectively with sonar. I think humans can do the same."

"Blue, that's quite brilliant," Dad said, and licked my face.

"Liza gave me the idea," I said, looking proudly at Liza.

"She's special."

"I love her."

"Do you love her as I love Rae?"

I wagged my tail and nodded.

Dad continued. "I think humans are already on a journey like dolphins, as you suggest, but in a simulated way, a virtual way with video games, directing their attention and improving their sentient capacity like little Michael and Kim with their video games. They direct their attention to visual and auditory areas of the brain while playing games, developing faster and more vigorous interactions in virtual environments, expanding their sentient capacity. Soon language-thinking will become less significant, and politicians will no longer dictate what humans are meant to become. A new era has dawned right in front of our noses, but it will take time to change the status quo."

My face lit up in amazement. "So it's not too late to save them from the self-destruction of their language-thinking political power struggles."

"It's not too late. I've decided humankind's journey to greater sentient awareness and greater freedom is underway, transcending the Progressive Socialists' ability to control Americans with language and propaganda like critical race theory. By expanding sentient capacity, humans will find truth and freedom much faster than by language-thinking. But we'll still need to save them from the immediate threat of Ripper, the Taliban, and the Old Man."

I smiled to myself. My dad had figured it out, what had been bothering me since I was a pup—how would I free human attention from their language-thinking prison. The answer had been right in front of my nose—little Michael's video games.

Walking on grass for the last couple of miles, my paws had stopped aching. I turned and grinned at Liza, Mom, then the rest of our troop. Trailing by thirty yards, Harry and Teak brought up the rear. I looked toward the sky and saw Doctor Biggs soaring near the clouds. Then I directed my attention to God in gratitude.

I'd found my meaning, and I knew in my heart that we'd find Michael, Kim, Nancy, and John and warn them about Ripper, the Taliban, and the Old Man's nuclear holocaust. Then I'd love my human family and help them direct their attention to sentient consciousness.

23

About three hours later, two Humvees approached. I barked, hoping they were Americans coming to take us to the US Embassy in Islamabad.

One vehicle drove past us, and the other stopped in front. I smelled a trap. The two guys driving looked like Harkoni's Taliban, wearing white turbans. I turned and yelled, "Run, run!"

Mom couldn't run, though, because she was exhausted and too close to delivery.

"Blue, run!" Dad yelled. "I'll stay with your mother."

I growled and barked, showing my teeth as two Taliban soldiers approached. One soldier shot off a couple of warning shots into the sky. I held my ground.

"Run, Blue," Mother cried.

Liza was running toward a group of trees, but she stopped and turned. "Blue, Blue!"

A shot rang out, echoing in my head. Time slowed down. I was hit. Yelping, I dropped to the ground, my head spinning.

I heard Dad's thunderous bark in a ferocious tone

like when the wolves attacked us. He charged the soldier who'd shot me, rose up, grabbed him by the throat, and knocked him down. Mom had the other soldier on the ground, her mouth around his neck. I heard our troops coming to our rescue, barking, and growling like a pack of wolves. I closed my eyes, relieved Mom and Dad would be okay.

Several moments passed, and I opened my eyes to say goodbye. The bullet had passed through my side, and Liza was licking the exit wound, which was still bleeding. Duke, Tiny, and George stood over me, like angels to the rescue. Mingus, Molly, and Teak licked my face. "I love you all," I said, feeling my life slipping away, drifting toward a bright light, filled with goodness and joy.

"No, no! Blue, Blue!" Liza screamed.

Dad bit my wound, pinching the skin and subcutaneous tissue together to stop the bleeding. Ten minutes passed, and my breathing slowly improved. Mom grabbed the loose skin at the nape of my neck, and she and Dad dragged me beneath a tree near a beautiful blue stream of water.

I opened my eyes wide, and Liza looked so sad. Mom's sad tears turned to joy as she watched life come back to my eyes. Liza smiled and licked my face. Dad still had my wound pinched between his teeth. I was so thirsty.

George, Duke, and Tiny produced loud barks of joy. Perched above in the tree, Doctor Biggs directed Dad on the hemostasis of my wound. Mom slid me over the grass to the stream where I wet my lips, drinking cool water that tasted better than any water I'd ever had, reminding me of Colonel the night I'd set him free, and Simone too.

Suddenly, for a moment I thought I could see Simone and Colonel walking toward me. Then Dad eased off on his bite, garnering my attention, and we found that the bleeding had stopped. Doctor Biggs told me not to move. Liza lay beside me, nudging me with her nose and licking me in love. Harry approached, his eyes filled with tears.

"I've never told you what Simone whispered into my ear on that special night when we all committed to not leaving anyone behind," Harry said, his voice trembling. "She said you better get off your knees because Blue saved us both. I love Simone, and I love you, Blue."

"No Paws Left Behind," I said, and hugged Harry as he cried. I whispered into his ear, "Simone is with us now in sentient reflection. We'll never forget her or Colonel." I closed my eyes out of exhaustion.

My thoughts raced, and horrific images of al-Qaeda's attack on America on September 11, 2001, played in my mind, only one hundred thousand times worse, with ashes everywhere and no skyscrapers anywhere in America, rocks and rubble everywhere. My attention visited every city in every state, and nothing was standing: no trees, no buildings, no homes. America had turned into a heap of ashes. The few survivors walked like zombies, pulling the dead behind them, themselves dying slowly from radiation poisoning. Then a TV lit up with an image of the Old Man and Ripper, and standing beside them Harkoni and Badass.

I woke with Liza licking my face and Mom and Dad looking down on me.

"You were dreaming, Blue," said Dad.

"I was having the worst nightmare ever. We've got to get to Islamabad."

"Doctor Biggs wants you to rest tonight," said Liza.

"We'll leave tomorrow morning," Mom said, and licked my forehead.

"Dad, promise me you'll talk to John and Nancy about the Old Man's nuclear holocaust," I said, lifting my head from the creek bank.

Dad checked my wound and reminded me not to move my torso. "We'll tell them together tomorrow. I promise on my name and life," he said softly.

Relieved, I relaxed my head into Liza's loving paws.

About the Author

C. S. Huxley is a catalyst, wit, scholar, inventor, Christian, and advocate for perennial Romanticism.